HEAVEN'S CALLED

Published by Dark Titan Entertainment.

Dark Titan Universe is a branch of Dark Titan Entertainment.

First Printing 2020.

Hardcover ISBN: 978-1-7353154-6-1
eBook ISBN: 978-1-7353154-7-8

darktitanentertainment.com

WORKS BY TY'RON W. C. ROBINSON II

BOOKS

DARK TITAN UNIVERSE SAGA

MAIN SERIES
Dark Titan Knights
The Resistance Protocol
Tales of the Scattered
Tales of the Numinous
Day of Octagon
Crossbreed
Heaven's Called

SPIN-OFFS
In A Glass of Dawn: The Casebook of Travis Vail
Maveth: Bloodsport

FORTHCOMING
The Curse of The Mutant-Thing
Trail of Vengeance
War of The Thunder Gods

FORTHCOMING
The Resistance/Protectors War
Underworld
Magicks and Mysticism
The Resistance vs. Enforcement Order

THE HAUNTED CITY SAGA
The Legendary Warslinger: The Haunted City I
Battle of Astolat: A Haunted City Prequel (KOBO Exclusive)
Redemption of the Lost: The Haunted City II
Consequences of the Suffering: The Haunted City III (Forthcoming)

SYMBOLUM VENATORES
Symbolum Venatores: The Gabriel Kane Collection
Hod: A Symbolum Venatores Book
Symbolum Venatores: War of The Two Kingdoms (Forthcoming)

OTHER BOOKS
Lost in Shadows: A Novel
Lost in Shadows: Remastered
Accounts of The Dead Days
The Book of The Elect
Dark Titan Omnibus: Volume 1
The Extended Age Omnibus
Frightened!: The Beginning
EverWar Universe: Knights & Lords (Forthcoming)
Dark Titan Omnibus: Volume 2 (Forthcoming)

DARK TITAN
UNIVERSE SAGA

HEAVEN'S CALLED

TY'RON W. C. ROBINSON II

CONTENTS

DARK TITAN ONE-SHOT
THE MYTHOLOGISTS

Jacob Wilson sat in the British Library of London, England. He sat at a table near the King's Library. Jacob is a frequent visitor of the library due to his time in school. Always near and within. Drinking a cup of coffee, sitting near him is a book on Oceania mythology. An avid reader of such histories, Jacob became well-verse in the art of understanding. His knowledge of mythologies stood superb.

While sipping his coffee and glancing through the pages of the book, a man approached the table. Well-dressed in a suit and middle-aged. Jacob looked up to him. His first thought was the man was an employee of the library, but his presence told a different story.

"I see you're into the Oceania myths."

"I am. Seeing how they compare to the others."

"Ah, you're trying to understand how they communicate with the Greeks? Or the Egyptians?"

"Maybe."

"Or you're trying to comprehend the Oceanic to the Maori or the Aboriginal Australians?"

"You know of them?"

"I do."

"It's interesting to speak with another who knows of them."

"Well, their gods aren't quite superior to those of the mainstream. Most of humanity prefer Odin or Zeus to give them a spark. Not the Oceanic ones."

"Then you know of the *Maui* and *Tawhaki* Cycles?"

"Of their tales of becoming heroes? I am deeply aware. So deep, that both Maui and Tawhaki represent the tendencies of the liberal and conservative within human beings."

Jacob nodded with a smirk.

"You know them well."

"I'm at the age where I know many things."

"How did you come into studying mythologies?"

"Myself and my crew, we're… well-versed in every mythology known to man and history."

"Your crew?"

"There are many of us. I just happen to be the one to grab the books for the study."

"I've never heard of a group of mythologists."

"It's a secret ordeal. Only a few are aware of such existence."

"Why?"

"Because, simply put, we cannot allow the base-minded of humanity to enter the doors. Otherwise, the group would tumble into the abyss."

"What if they wanted to prove themselves? To see if they could join?"

"Then, they would be where you are right now. You have the knowledge. The mindset. The skills of study. You would fit well alongside us. Our purpose is the key."

"Purpose?"

"I cannot speak of such things in the public forum. However, I will give you an invite to one of our meetings being held tonight here in London."

The man handed Jacob a card. Looked as if it was a business card, However, upon the card was an address and an insignia. Jacob stared hard at the symbol.

"I've never seen this symbol before. What is it?"

"You'll find out if you agree to come."

Jacob took another look at the card.

"It's your call." The man said.

Jacob placed the card in his pocket, he looked up and the man was gone. Nowhere in sight.

"Huh." Jacob uttered under his breath.

When nightfall had come, Jacob went to the location listed on the card. Finding himself walking on the grounds of the Middle Temple in the City of London. Unsure he would be granted entry, he noticed those around him didn't approach him. They didn't cease him nor did they try to stop him. They all nodded. Jacob felt strange by such responses. All silent in sound, but very loud in action. Jacob entered the Temple, walking into the Hall.

Inside, sat a long rectangular table and around it were twelve individuals. Seven men and five women. All ranged in different nationalities and cultures. Jacob was still, he looked out and saw the man he met in the library and walked over toward him.

"Excuse me, sir."

The man looked and saw Jacob. A smile appeared upon his face.

"You decided to come."

"Yes, I didn't know such a thing like this existed."

"Well, you're seeing another view of the world. One not many will ever have the opportunity to see."

The man gestured for Jacob to sit at the table, which everyone else was doing. Jacob sat next to the man as they were served dinner. The table was covered in dishes, each one came from another culture in the world. The diversity was clear in the group. Jacob was amazed. They ate and afterwards, the table was cleared of the food and out came the books. Thick books, very old with worn-out leather binding. Some of the books were written in Old English, Persian, Latin, and Aramaic. Jacob felt as if he was in another world. His eyes gazing at the books. Books hundreds, perhaps thousands of years old. The man leaned in over to him, sliding over a book.

"I think you'll be interested in this one."

Jacob grabbed the book. No title was on the cover, Jacob opened it and saw the words were written in *Paleo-Hebrew*. He shook his head.

"How did you come across something such as this?"

"We have our ways."

"This language? I thought it was only written on scrolls."

"Things the world has been taught are not what they seem."

"What do you mean?"

"Look around. See all of us in this hall. We come from different parts of the world, yet we share the same values and goals. To make this world better for the generations to come. This is how we start. By restoring what has been lost."

'Then, why is this a secret. How come you don't tell the public about this?"

"If we were to do such a thing, it would put a target on our heads. Not only of the natural, but of the others."

"Others? Like governments?"

"Higher than governments." The man nodded. "Come with me to the library. I'll explain everything there."

Jacob followed the man into the library of the Temple. It was only the two of them, surrounded by more of the books the others were gazing through. Jacob also saw the globes designed by Emery Molyneux.

"It's better you sit for what I am about to tell you."

Jacob sat down at the table. The man stood by the wall and reached into his jacket pocket, taking out a cigar and lit up. Inhaling and exhaling.

"You can smoke in here?"

"It's our place. We are obliged to. Cigars for the most part, of course."

The man took another puff of the cigar before sitting down in front of Jacob.

"The truth of such a group as this is simple, yet complex. It only depends on the mind of the listener."

"I'm listening."

The man nodded with a smile.

"Good. This group is no ordinary group. We're a secret society. Kept hidden from most of the world because our purpose is deemed tyrannical and cynical to most of the general public."

"Tyrannical?"

"We do not wish to enslave humanity. Only to open their eyes to the true ways of the world."

"I noticed one of the books on the table was a grimoire."

"It's good you did. I'm sure that gives you a better understanding as to what and who we are."

"You all practice magic?"

"Some do. Myself, I stick only with history and the power of the ancients. When I said governments and the public would try to shut us down. I didn't tell you the other half of the story."

"And that half would be?"

"The deities you read about. The ones in all the mythologies. They exist."

Jacob sat back in the chair, rubbing his chin and gazing around the library. He leaned in toward the table.

"I'm not understanding. How? It makes no sense."

"To the natural mind of man, it does not. However, what we have discovered over many centuries, is these mythologies we've come to know them as just stories. Tales of legends and fables. But, what we have learned is the true fact. These tales are not myths. The legends are real. The accounts are real. It all happened."

"Where's the proof?" Jacob asked. "How can I believe you if I haven't seen them myself?"

The man nodded.

"The risen heroes."

"Can't be. They're not like the gods in the myths."

"Are you sure about that? Look at them. Their feats. Their power. The things they can do and have done. They are the purest sign of the tide turning. The heroes shall come first and the gods come after. The heroes are here and the world is aware of them. We now, wait upon the gods to make themselves known."

"Now, I'm curious. Have any of you met one of these heroes or the gods?"

"No. but, our leader has met with something from the other side."

"You speak of the supernatural."

"Yes. That is what I was referring to when I spoke about opposition. The supernatural realm doesn't take our society too well. There are a particular few who desire us to disappear. For their good purpose."

"Who are they?"

"Their names I do not know. I know only what the ancients had called them. There were three. One was deemed the Hunter of the Realms. He carried wrath wherever he went. The second one was referred to as Haunting Wanderer. He would always appear when there was someone in dire need. Be it near-death or near-revelation."

"And the third?"

"He was called by many names. But, the one that has stuck with me is the Keeper of the Cosmos. He controls all the darkness in the universe. An Astral entity. He is one I dare not to come across."

"What happens if you do?"

'Then, it will be the end of the Mythologists. Period."

Jacob took in the information and kept it close. He glanced at his watch, amazed by the time which had gone by.

"I need to get home."

"Understood."

Jacob stood up and so did the man. He extended his hand toward Jacob.

"It was a pleasure to meet you, Jacob.

Jacob shook his hand in respect.

"I have to ask, you never told me your name."

"Ah. The society calls me Deimos."

"As in the Greek God?"

"It's what they've given me." The man replied. "Best be seeing you."

Jacob nodded and left the Temple.

Inside the library, Deimos sat still as another individual entered. He was cloaked in a white robe and hood. Deimos gazed upon him and bowed his head.

"I wasn't aware you would be here."

"I'm always near. What of you talks with the young lad?"

"He's very intelligent. I believe he can become one of us."

"Very well. Keep an eye on him."

"Yes sir."

While Jacob walked home, he found it strange there was no one else outside. No sign of any vehicles of any kind. Finding it weird, he began to move faster. Upon his footsteps, a peculiar mist arose from the ground.

Jacob looked in fear and immediately he turned around, finding himself staring at an entity. Dressed in a dark blue cloak, suit, and hat. His eyes clear with no pupils, yet they were glowing and shined bright as the moon. His facial hair and long hair were white as snow.

"Who are you?"

"I am one of the three Deimos told. I was known as the Haunting Wanderer in the times past. Now, humanity refers to me as he Visitant Outlander."

Jacob stood still. Fear grabbed him.

"Do not fear me, Jacob Wilson. For I am not of the malevolent side of life."

Jacob calmed down. The fear which held him had evaporated.

"Why have you come to me?"

"To give you a revelation. Your life is about to change, Jacob. The life you shall live will be drastically different than the lives of the average. You will suffer loss and you will receive gain. You will come across those of a good nature like myself and others present in evil."

"Are the Mythologists evil?"

"They're neutral. But, their goals conflict with the laws of the true nature. The spiritual realms deem them cinderblocks into the hearts and minds of the faithful. That shall not happen to you."

"How do you know?"

"Because I know the end from the beginning. I've seen your life up till now. The lives of others. I've interacted with a few of the risen heroes and others such as yourself. You will receive a change soon. Best to be prepared."

The mist evaporated and the Visitant Outlander disappeared. Jacob turned around at the sound of a horn, seeing a car pass by. Around him were other vehicles and pedestrians. Jacob scratched his head, turning back and forth.

"What I have gotten myself into?"

JACOB WILL BE SEEN AGAIN AND THE MYTHOLOGISTS WILL RETURN

CREED: MEDIEVAL TIMES

I

VISITATION

Creed mediated in the clouds during the night. His eyes closed, the aura of his power surging around him as his cloak bellowed with the moving air. From behind him, a loud bang sounded, getting his attention. Once Creed's eyes opened, he turned back seeing what had caused the sound and from its location appeared a very bright light. The light was brighter than the sun, yet its brightness had no effect on Creed. Within the light, Creed saw a figure approaching. He raised himself up, levitating in the air as the figure emerged from the light.

"You." Creed said.

"It's time we've met."

The figure appeared like a woman. Elderly in age. She was clothed in a long black dress, decorated with rubies, sapphires, and emeralds within the lining. She also wore a medallion made of platinum with a carbuncle gem. Her flowing white hair shined with the light as did her white eyes which glowed in similar fashion.

"Why have you come, Madam Age?"

"To give you a warning. Someone is coming."

"Let me guess. Adrambadon is crawling back up from the Cryptic Zone?"

"No. He is currently occupied with other matters."

"Then, who is coming?"

"Medieval is coming."

"Medieval?"

"You are aware of him, aren't you? The knightly figure that caused the massacres throughout the Middle Ages. He's the one responsible for the Crusades. All of them."

"Why is he coming here?"

"He's looking for you."

"For me?"

"You prove to him as a great challenge. You remind him of another."

"I guess this other one didn't get the task done."

"He did. Just that was hundreds of years in human time."

"How soon will this Medieval figure be here?"

"Very soon. I've informed Ananchel about the circumstance. She will meet with you soon and give you the other details."

"Other details? Why won't you tell me?"

"It's not my duty. It's hers."

Madam Age walked back into the light and as she did, the portal closed and the light dimmed out. Behind Creed appeared Ananchel, flying down from the heavens. The two greeted one another before Ananchel noticed the last remnants of Madam Age's portal.

"She already told you?"

"Said you have something else to add." Creed mentioned. "What is it?"

"I have some information on Medieval. He's moving with great energy and speed outside the realms of time and space from the Middle Ages. That's how he's making his way here."

"Then why don't those on the outside stop him from breaching into our time?"

"They have matters of their own."

"I'm sure someone is watching."

"Oh, they are. But, it's complicated as you are aware."

"I comprehend. What must I do to ensure this Medieval figure doesn't cause any harm?"

"Simply wait for him to make himself known."

"Why not just stop him in his tracks?"

"Because, when he does show up, he's coming for you. You're the reason for his arrival. Not Adrambadon or Demonticronto. He wants to face you."

"Madam Age said he's after me because of another in his time."

"Yes. Another Creed from the Middle Ages."

"Another Creed?"

"I know this is a lot to deal with. But, right now, just prepare yourself for Medieval's arrival."

"I can't just sit here in the air and wait for him."

"It wouldn't do any good anyway. Medieval can't fly or levitate. He's ground-based. You'll have to meet him upon the soil."

"Where must I go to ensure there are no innocents in the surroundings?"

"Head to a peculiar cemetery in the west. There, you'll meet a man called the Caretaker. He's dealt with Medieval before and I know he'll give you some advice on him."

"The Caretaker."

"Yes. You two should get along well."

Ananchel hovered higher into the air above creed. Looking up toward the heavens.

"I must know about this other Creed you've mentioned."

"In time." Ananchel said before flying off.

II

ANCIENT TALES

Creed appeared in the cemetery, which was far further west from his current location. Creed walked upon the grounds, passing by the dozens of headstones and statues. Tall figures of angels in the catholic fashion. Other statues were those of Freemasonry. Brotherhoods and Sisterhoods. Creed's cloak flowed with the incoming gusts of wind. He walked further and saw a man standing still, a shovel in his hand.

"Are you the Caretaker?" Creed asked.

"Who wants to know?"

"That's why I asked."

The man turned around, facing Creed. Creed saw his face. One of an elder. He wore a wide brim hat and a black duster. He stuck the shovel into the ground and approached Creed with a stillness in his eyes. Yet, there was life in them. A lot of life.

"You're him aren't you?" The man said. "The Unholy Knight."

"I am. I suspect you must be the Caretaker."

"Correct. Ananchel already told me everything that's going on. Right now, we need to discuss the proper planning."

"Do you know who Medieval is?"

"I am familiar with him. However, he's not human as some of the stories tell. He's a spirit. A spirit which thrived during the second and third crusades."

"He's never been a mortal."

"Although, he shares their desires and their lusts. He craves war. In the Templar texts, he was referred to as a god of war."

"I never assumed I would be up against a god. Nonetheless, a war god."

"Now, since we are aware of Medieval's arrival, the strategy is to face him head-on."

"Head-on?" Creed asked. "Just the two of us?"

"I've heard of the things you've done. Facing the likes of Adrambadon and Demonticronto. My friend, you are capable of facing Medieval on your own."

"Noted. Perhaps I should do that."

"It's what Madam Age wants." Caretaker added. "She sees you as a powerful force who can combat the darker entitles at work. You're different than the other Creeds who've come before you."

"Ananchel told me you've dealt with Medieval yourself in times past."

"I did."

"What happened?"

"It was during the third Crusade. I was a member of the Knights Hospitaller. During the battle in Acre, Medieval appeared on the field and slaughtered all the Muslim forces of Saladin, giving way for us to achieve victory. But, that wasn't his desire. He attacked all of us and killed many. I fought against him with three of my brothers-in-arms. I alone survived the attack and sent Medieval on his way back into the spirit realm."

"You defeated him?"

"My skill set was enough to keep me alive. Medieval saw my integrity and grit as a badge of honor. He let me live."

"Will he do it again?"

"Probably not. It won't be the same this time."

"I have to ask. What is all of this about other Creeds?"

"You're one in many. During the Crusades, there was one. He stayed to himself and only appeared when there was a battle to be won. He was a mystery and still is."

Creed looked over near one of the headstones and saw a quickening shadow dash right before his eyes. Creed stood his guard as the Caretaker saw his stance.

"What is it?"

"We're not alone out here." Creed said. "Someone else is watching us. Closely."

From behind Creed, the shadow bolted like lightning, striking Creed and knocking him into the Caretaker. The two fell to the ground and Creed looked up, seeing the shadow figure molding into a physical form. Upon its body was the armor of a knight. 14th Century armor in detail. Covered in a black and worn-out tunic with no insignias or shields pertaining to any kingdom or country. He wielded a sword.

"Is that him?" Creed asked.

"No. That's not Medieval. But, he's dressed like it."

Caretaker stepped forward to face the entity with Creed's cloak surrounding the area. His shovel in hand.

"What's your name, spirit?" Caretaker asked.

"My name?" The spirit said with a hallowing voice.

"Yeah. You have a name. What is it?"

"My master calls me Middle Age."

"Middle Age?" Caretaker paused. "As in one from the period?"

"It is what I am."

"You don't belong here. Take your sword and walk on out of this cemetery."

"I cannot. For I have come under commands. To send you both elsewhere."

"Where's Medieval?" Creed asked.

"You'll see him soon. Right now, you must go there."

"Go where?"

"I'll show you."

Middle Age raised up his sword, striking the air, thus creating a rift between time and space. Caretaker looked on as did Creed. Middle Age turned toward them as the dark blue hue from the rift grew.

"Where does this go?" Caretaker asked.

"It goes where my master wants you to go."

"Alright, you smartass."

Middle Age took his sword and swiped the end of it against Caretaker's back, knocking him into the rift. Creed swooped over and grabbed the sword. Middle Age laughed before pushing creed into the rift himself. After entering the rift, Creed and Caretaker find themselves falling down within a portal. They collapse onto the grounds of somewhere else. Somewhere far from the cemetery. Creed stood up and looked around.

"Where are we?"

Caretaker stood on his feet and observed the surroundings. He knew.

"Ah shit."

"What?"

"I know where we are."

"How do you know?"

Caretaker pointed ahead of them. Creed looked out and saw bodies of knights on the ground. Blood covering their armor. Some wore the crests of the Knights Templar.

"We're in the past." Caretaker said.

"The past?"

"We're in the medieval times now."

"If I may ask, what year?"

"1202."

III

1202 AD

Creed and Caretaker walked over the field of bodies while hearing the clashing echoes of swords in the distance. With the sound of swords were screams. All of which were in a rage.

"We need to reach the battle." Caretaker said.

"Let me have a look."

Creed hovered himself into the air, passing over the trees and stone walls to see the battle before his eyes. What Creed saw was a battle of the Crusades. The Knights Templar were fighting against the Muslims. A gruesome sight to see. Creed wasn't bothered by the falling limbs and bodies. Blood covered the grounds.

"What do you see?" Caretaker asked.

"Templars. Muslims. This is a Crusades' battle."

Creed looked closer into the armies of men, finding Middle Age in the midst of the battle, killing both Templars and Muslims without being seen by the human eye.

"Middle Age is there!"

"Good. We need to get to him fast."

"Allow me."

Creed grabbed Caretaker by his arm and flew over the walls and into the middle of the battle. Quickly they were caught into the attacks of the Templars and Muslims. In the fighting, Creed fell a strange disturbance in the air. Something familiar to himself. What he was sensing wasn't Middle Age nor was it Medieval himself.

"What is it?" Caretaker asked, after impaling a Templar with his own sword.

"There's another Creed here."

"Ah. I know who you're talking about."

Caretaker looked out and saw him. Riding into battle on an armored horse was a knight. This knight's features were highly similar to Creed's own appearance. Only exceptions were the helmet and the armor. The knight jumped from his mount and crashed into the battlefield, fighting against the Muslims in such a quick succession. Creed watched him fight. Using familiar tactics of his own. Creed could even sense the Cryptic Zone's power upon him.

"He's a Creed."

"One of many." Caretaker said. "There are some things you've yet to learn."

During the Knightcreed's onslaught, another mysterious entity bolted out into the battle on a flaming horse. The flames were not the color of the average fire. These flames glowed with a bright white and blue. The rider himself was dressed in royal garbs covered with armor. His face appeared as a burning skull.

"A Chaser." Caretaker uttered.

"You're aware of them."

"Oh yes. I never suspected one to have been around during this era."

While the two fought in the field, Middle Age appeared before Creed and Caretaker. His sword in hand, ready for the fight.

"Why did you send us here?" Caretaker asked.

"I have my orders."

"I will ask once again. Where's Medieval?"

"He's here." Middle Age answered, moving to the side.

Walking up behind Middle Age was a figure, dressed in beaten and burnt armor. His face covered by the appearance of a skull. His footsteps made the sound of clashing metal. He stood at the height of Creed, yet was leaner.

"I am Medieval."

"I see you're still roaming around this era." Caretaker said. "Why?"

"Because it is where I thrive. Many souls have fallen to my blade. Yours should've been one of them."

"Turned out differently as I recall."

Medieval looked over toward Creed. He scoffed with a nod.

"You're him."

"Who am I?"

"The one they've sent to eliminate me."

"You know of it?"

"I'm a spirit. Time is only a means of travel to my kind."

"Then, you know why I'm on your trail."

"I do. Now, shall we begin?"

Medieval pulled out a shotgun from behind, aimed at Creed. The shot emitted a powerful blast, knocking both Creed and Caretaker back, but Creed felt the blow, causing a major wound on his chest. Caretaker rose up, seeing Creed holding his chest as the reddish-orange blood poured from it.

"Never in my existence have I ever saw the Cryptic-blood pour from one's body. It is something to behold."

IV

<u>THERE'S NOTHING NEW</u>

"Why use such a weapon during this age?" Caretaker asked. "Why not just run toward us with a sword?!"

"Because it is too simple. A weapon such as this is profound in this era. A rightful choice in war."

"I've had enough listening to him speak." Creed said.

"I'm not finished yet." Medieval replied, shooting toward Creed.

Creed moved himself out of the blast range with the strength he still wielded. Medieval sighed. Caretaker circled the enemy and from behind him appeared Middle Age, tripping the Caretaker to the ground. More of the Templar knights and Muslims ran into the foreground where they stood, covering Creed and Caretaker from their sights. Medieval commanded Middle Age to find them. While doing so, Medieval blasted all those who stood in his path, walking through the battle shooting both templars and Muslims. Caretaker carried Creed from the battlefield, laying him aside near a ravaged home. Caretaker saw the wound, it's still bleeding, not as much as before.

"You need to find a way to heal fast."

"I'm doing all I can. What weapon was that?"

"A shotgun."

"That was no simple shotgun. It took me down. Made me bleed. It has to be a weapon made by Adrambadon or someone in the same vain."

The trampling of a horse is heard near the home and came to a solid stop. Creed and Caretaker were awaiting to see who the rider could be and the door of the home opened. Caretaker saw him and Creed wondered with questions.

"Caretaker?" The rider said.

"Yes. I see you remember me."

"I do. Why does he have my likeness?"

"Why do you have mine?" Creed asked, staring at the Knight Creed.

"I see now. He's from another time. How far out?"

"From the future. Approximately eight-hundred and eighteen years."

"The Cryptic Lineage continues further I see. Well, no matter for the cause. He's wounded greatly."

"He just needs a moment to heal."

"I will handle it."

Knight Creed walked over and knelt in the presence of Creed. Placing his right hand upon Creed's chest and without a moment's notice, the wound was healed. Caretaker was astonished by the quickness of the process.

"I never knew you could heal others."

"It comes and goes. Mainly a cause for the battles."

Knightcreed helped Creed to his feet and the two gave a nod of exchange.

"Why are you both here in this era?"

"We were brought here by Middle Age. He's working with Medieval."

"You're saying what we're doing right now has no affect on the events of the future concerning Medieval?"

"They have affects. Just for a moment in time."

"You can't stay here any longer. The more you linger, the quicker you cause yourself to evaporate from the timeline."

"We don't know how to get back." Caretaker said.

"I will aid you. I have an ally who's out here that can transcend time and space. He'll be your way out of here."

"Where is he at the moment?"

"Battling the Muslims. He's Lord Klarson."

"Klarson?" Caretaker questioned. "I thought he was away when the battle took place."

"No. he's here and his fighting. With power that frightens those who don't believe."

Creed walked toward the door, passing by Caretaker and Knightcreed.

"Let's find him and get going."

"He takes after our kind." Knight Creed said.

"A little too much." Caretaker added.

Walking outside, seeing the battle continuing. Caretaker looked further, finding both Medieval and Middle Age. He pointed toward them, giving the notice to Creed and Knight Creed. Medieval continued blasting knights and Middle Age wandered around the dead bodies, checking their faces under the helmets.

"I see them." Knightcreed said, mounting his horse. "Follow my path and I will lead you to Lord Klarson."

"Will do." Creed replied.

Knightcreed rode off into the battlefield with Creed and Caretaker following. Right in the battle, Knight Creed took down several Muslims and Templar knights, giving an open pathway to Creed and Caretaker. While doing so, Middle Age gazed up from the ground over the dead bodies, seeing Creed and Caretaker. He pointed and let out a loud scream, giving the signal to Medieval, who saw them ahead.

"They're mine." Medieval spoke to himself.

Medieval ran with a mighty speed, bolting through the knights and Middle Age followed. Knight Creed led them up a hill, where they stood a small and sturdy temple. Walking out of the temple was Lord Klarson.

"The Chaser I saw." Creed said.

"Lord Klarson." Knight Creed said. "These two need your assistance."

"My assistance on what causes?"

"They need to return to their own time. They come from the future."

"The future? Yes. I see. It explains your doppelganger."

Klarson led them into the temple, where at the forefront was what looked to be a mirror. Nearly thirteen-feet in height and five-feet wide. Creed and Caretaker stood in front of the mirror as Klarson circled it. Knight Creed stood at the door, waiting for Medieval and Middle Age to arrive. Klarson whipped out a strange, sharp chain and he began to twirl it in the face of the mirror. The glass started to warp, forming a wormhole. Klarson's face turned into a skull, covered with sin fire. He pulled the chain back and pointed.

"Walk through and you shall return to your time."

Knight Creed looked out and saw Medieval and Middle Age rushing toward the temple. He grabbed his battle axe, telling Creed and Caretaker he and Klarson will hold them off. Caretaker nodded in a bid of farewell.

"Young one." Knight Creed said toward Creed. "Keep the faith. Never falter in the presence of your enemies."

"I will stand." Creed replied.

They stepped into the wormhole, hearing the clashing battle between Knight Creed and Klarson against Medieval and Middle Age. Medieval caught a slight glance at Creed entering the wormhole and screamed with anger.

"This is not over!"

Entering the wormhole, Creed and Caretaker are thrown back into their time period, right in the cemetery where they previously stood. Caretaker let out a sigh of relief.

"We're back."

"I see." Creed replied. "Although, something's off."

'What do you mean?"

"I can sense the Cryptic Zone. I sense Adrambadon. He's near."

DEATH CHASER-THE DEAL

I

REPENTANCE IS NIGH

It was a late night, elsewhere in a deserted landscape. Only the moon could be present in the midst of the barren grounds. The Death Chaser moved through the land, searching for his next target. A target which may indicate Demonticronto's apparent return. The Chaser did not utter a word.

In another location, John Clarkson continued his training with Widow by his side. He began teaching her the knowledge of the supernatural and the skills to fight against the demonic forces. The Chaser told John to instruct Widow in these ways to increase her faith and the chances for her survival in this world.

Between the physical and spiritual realms of existence, an entity emerged and stepped foot upon the earth. He was tall, dressed in black with dark-blue flashes of light emitting from his face. Only his eyes were as red as blood. Behind him stood three figures, shrouded in the shadows.

"We've arrived." The figure said. "Now, we find this Chaser and put him in his place."

"What of his allies?" Another figure asked.

"What about them? If they get in our way, we take them out. Simple."

"What if they do not?" Another figure questioned. "We leave them be?"

"Yes. We're only here for the Chaser. No one else."

"As you have spoken."

"That I have. Now, the three of you will travel to separate locations. I will give out the signal to bring the Chaser to each of you. Once, he is in your sights, eliminate him. If you fail, I hope the next one succeeds. We must take him out before Demonticronto makes his return."

"We will not fail."

"For your sakes. I hope not."

The three figures turned into mists and flowed above in the air, scattering themselves from Dieheart's presence. Dieheart smirked, holding out his arms with his hands wide open. He closed his eyes and exhaled.

"Soul of Retribution. There is a need that requires your aid. These locations are in need of your acquaintance. Go there. Do your work."

The Chaser continued moving through the desert and while on the move, he looked up, catching a bright flash of light. The light exploded and went into three separate paths. The Chaser knew of the light and the paths it made. He turned his focus from Demonticronto to the three paths and quickly made a right turn, heading toward the first path.

II
THE EARTH LIVETH

The Chaser had found himself after the traveling facing the Grand Canyon. He looked upon the structure of the area and saw a silhouette standing atop the Canyon. Even through the night sky, the Chaser keened his eyes and saw the form of the figure. He knew it wasn't human and stopped himself, pointing toward the figure.

"Whatever you proclaim yourself to be," The Chaser spoke. "Come down and face me."

The figure made its way to the ground to face the Chaser. As it stepped foot on the ground, the two entities shared a stare down. The Chaser could now see what the figure is and he nodded and pointed.

"You don't belong on this plane, demon."

"As a matter of fact, I don't. however, I was brought here in an urgent matter."

"Who sent you here?"

"A friend."

"The name of your friend?"

"You'll find out soon. If you can survive this battle."

"You threaten me?"

"It is my nature."

The Chaser stretched forth his hands and from them emerged the sinfire. The demon grinned, stepping back and raising his own arms, causing the ground to tremble. The Chaser kept his stance and his gaze focused.

"By the way, Chaser. I didn't tell you my name." The demon said. "I am Mineron, the Demon of the Earth."

"Never heard of you."

"Now you have."

Mineron raised up the dirt from the ground, forming it into a boulder. The dirt fell above the Chaser as he moved from the incoming attack. The Chaser rolled over the incoming boulder, turning toward Mineron and blasting him with the sinfire. Mineron brushed of the fire and smirked.

"I am made from the earth you see around you, Chaser." He taunted. "Fire cannot harm me!"

"So you believe." The Chaser replied. "Yet, you are not aware of how the things of the earth are made. What can change them and what can shape them. Yet, I am aware of such matters. This day, you will learn what happens to the earth when it feels the touch of brimstone."

Mineron levitated in the air above the Chaser with his arms stretched out and a large grin on his graveled face.

"Do your best!"

"I shall."

The Chaser twirled his hands and arms in a circle, conjuring the sinfire once more. He kept twirling as the circle grew in size and the flames brightened. Mineron crossed his arms and scoffed at the sight of the flaming circle. The chaser continued until the flames were in between himself and Mineron. The flames were the height of thirteen feet.

"What more is this?" Mineron asked. "What good does a jester trick do to stop me?"

"This is not a trick," The Chaser answered. "but a test. One you have failed."

"I'm ending this." Mineron dove down toward the Chaser.

"Yes, this is the end." The Chaser said, blasting the flaming circle toward Mineron.

Mineron flew directly in the circle and within mere seconds, his body was consumed by the flames. Mineron fell to the ground as the flames did not ceased and the circle started to close itself with Mineron in its grasp. Mineron struggled to get free, but the flames were like a tight band. Mineron couldn't stand up due to the circle as the Chaser walked over toward him, staring him down.

"Is this it?" Mineron asked. "What more must be done?"

"This is your end." The Chaser said. "You are done."

The Chaser waved his right hand and the flames consumed Mineron to the point his body became like magma, pouring from his eyes, ears, nose, and mouth. The Chaser saw Mineron's body melt and quickly freeze. At that point, the Chaser stomped Mineron's head into ashes and left his remains to burn in the sinfire. The Chaser left the Grand Canyon. While leaving, thunder cracked from above with a strange laughter following. The chaser looked up and felt the same energy that was within Mineron coming from the clouds above.

"Another one." The Chaser said.

III

STORMS OF THE AIR

While the Chaser sought after what was roaming in the skies above, John and Widow traveled into a small town. While tracking the source, Widow spotted a place where it read "Fortune Telling" above the doors. She stopped, pointing toward it as John gave a look.

"What about it?"

"We should go in there. See what they know."

"You already know that's not a wise move."

"How come? We need to find out if Demonti is returning soon. Perhaps, the fortune teller inside knows of it."

"There's no need for it. The Chaser will tell us everything when the time is near."

"What if it's hidden from him as well? Look, let's go in there, ask about Demonti, and see what we find. Afterwards, we'll leave and give our results to the Chaser."

John shook his head, looking back and forth between the building and Widow.

"This is on you if something goes wrong."

"I already know. I'll take my judgment justly."

They entered the building. Seeing its walls covered with gems and crystals. Near them in the front was a round table, carved with magical symbols relating to the elements of the earth. Widow approached the table, seeing the markings while John walked around the place, searching for someone. Anyone.

"Is anyone in here?" John asked. "We're at this table. Letting you know."

From the back walked out a young woman. Dressed in a violet dress from her chest to feet. She brushed back her black wavy hair as she approached John and Widow.

"I see visitors this night. I wasn't aware they'll be you."

"What do you mean?" John questioned.

"I knew you were coming here. You work alongside a Chaser."

"Yes." Widow said. "Yes, we do."

"Then, you are aware of why we're here."

"I am. You desire to find answers regarding Demonticronto's imminent return."

"Well, is he returning soon." John asked.

"Please, sit and I shall explain everything to you."

John sat at the table besides Widow while the young woman sat in front of them. She giggled.

"Forgive my manners, my name is Madame LoCasta."

"How long have you done this type of work?" John wondered. "You seem a bit young to be capable of this."

"I was born into this life. Grew up in the arts. Trust me, I am capable of accomplishing what to seek."

The Chaser moved into the skies through the fiery whirlwind and ceased himself in the air. Covered within the dark clouds and seeing quick flashes of lightning surrounding him. He could hear the mumblings of a voice.

"Show yourself, spirit."

A gust of wind blew toward the Chaser, not fazing him nor stumbling him. From there a small whirlwind appeared before him and formed into the image of a man. Yet, this form had the appearance of a man with uncertain features. Reptile-like eyes, long dark wavy and sharp hair. His teeth were like a tiger's and the nails on his fingers resembled claws. His skin was a pale blue. Yet, darker than the morning sky.

"Who are you?" The Chaser asked.

"I am Shinow. The Demon of the Air. Bringer of Storms."

"Who sent you?"

"You will know in good time."

"Your ally said the same before I ended him."

"There's only three of us and yet, you've managed to take one of us out? He didn't tell us you had such strength."

"Who is he?"

"The one who sent us."

"Enough talk, I'm going to finish you off for invading this realm."

"You can try. For one cannot catch the wind."

The Chaser scoffed and from his hands emerged the sinfire and with it he tossed it into the clouds surrounding himself and Shinow. Shinow summoned the wind, seeking to remove the fire, yet the fire was no kindled by Shinow's power. The Chaser bowed his head and a lightning bolt came from behind him, traveling through the clouds and striking the sin fire. Creating a vacuum of flames, burning the air within. Therefore, suffocating Shinow. Shinow raised his hands and rain started to fall from above. The rain was not enough to take out the flames as it had no affect.

"What is this?!" Shinow yelled. "My powers cannot contain the flames!"

"Because the flames burn all that has the residue of sin." The Chaser said. "You, demon of the air are consumed by sin. Therefore, you must burn."

Shinow yelled greatly as the sinfire consumed him. Burning him into nothing more than floating ashes of light. The Chaser sighed as he heard a distant voice higher than the clouds.

"The firmament."

Madame LoCasta sat still at the table while John and Widow waited patiently for an answer. Any answer. LoCasta opened her eyes and they were red as blood. Her pupils could not be seen and it frightened Widow, yet John was not afraid.

"I know you're not LoCasta. Who are you?"

"I am the one you seek." A deep voice said out of LoCasta's mouth with a grin.

"Demonti?" Widow said.

"You believe you can trace my actions. You sought after my patterns and it's led you here. To sit at the feet of a sorceress. What would the Chaser think of you now?"

"We're here on business. Not on some wicked adventure."

"Keep telling yourselves such lies. In time, we shall meet in the flesh. But for now, I wait until the time is appointed and I am called."

"We will stop you." John said. "When the time does come."

"We shall see. But, for now, I suggest you focus on the enemy at hand."

"Enemy?"

"Right at the door."

John turned around, hearing the front door open. He turned back to LoCasta, seeing her eyes have reverted to their natural state and Demonticronto was gone. John looked and saw who was approaching.

"Well, it seems I've just missed my chance to seek some answers."

"And you are?" John asked. "One of Demonti's dogs?"

"No. I am Dieheart. One who has worked with Demonticronto ever since the days began."

"Why are you here?" LoCasta asked. "Do you seek something of value?"

"I'm here to finally see the Chaser's allies. Fitting they'll be in a place like this. Unbeknownst to the Chaser himself."

"I suggest you watch yourself. He could show up here at any moment."

"I'm afraid not. I'm too wise to fall for the tricks of man. The Chaser is currently preoccupied with several of my own forces. Which leaves the two of you alone with me."

"We can handle ourselves."

"I'm sure you can. No need to prepare for a fight. I only came to see you as a warning. Remove yourself from this path or suffer much dire consequences."

"I think not." John said, stepping up to Dieheart. "We will live and die on this path. For The Chaser has shown us what must be done in these last days."

Dieheart nodded, grinning as he crested his chin.

"I see. Very well. When the time does arrive, I hope you're prepared for a quick death."

Dieheart turned and left LoCasta's place. She turned to John and Widow, sighing.

"Did you get all you came for?"

"That and a little more." John replied.

"Thank you." Widow said.

IV

THE SEAS OF THE FIRMAMENT

The Chaser went high into the atmosphere, reaching the second heaven. Looking out toward the sun and the moon across from one another, he listened closely once more, hearing the strange noises coming from higher above. Much higher than the stars around him.

"Is it possible?" The Chaser questioned to himself. "If it is such, this is not a matter of my own. But of the others."

From there, a voice echoed from above the Chaser, speaking in such language familiar to the demons he faced earlier. There, the Chaser knew he was dealing with another demon. However, this one was sitting above the firmament. The Chaser keened his flaming eyes, setting them clearly to focus. Upon focusing, he saw the demon in the waters above. Nearly camouflaged with the darkness.

"You do not belong up there, demon."

"This is the perfect place to settle this business. I'm sure the others won't be bothered by the battle."

"You have trespassed a place beyond your borders!"

The Chaser rushed himself into the seas above. Now covered by the waters and shrouded in the darkness. The demon was invisible to the Chaser's eyes, yet his flaming eyes did not evaporate. The Chaser swam through the waters, he couldn't even seethe second heaven beneath him, except for the piercing dim light near the top of the waters.

"Show yourself." The Chaser spoke.

Right in front of him, the demon morphed from the waters. Creating itself a body from the waters. The demon's appearance was very similar to Shinow, only for the hair to be flowing with water. The Chaser stopped himself, lifting his body upright to face the demon.

"Who are you?" The Chaser asked.

"My name is Flrange. This is my domain."

"Your domain? No demons are allowed to dwell in these parts."

"And you speak for the authority?"

"I speak for those who cannot speak. As they cannot speak such words."

"Go about your business or else I must deal with you swiftly."

"I have come to you to send you into the pit where you belong. With the others."

"You speak of Shinow and Mineron. I am aware of their defeat by your hand. The dealmaker told me of the events."

"Dealmaker?"

"We were sent here by a very powerful ally. To see if you were truly as Demonticronto and the others have said you to be."

"Who is this dealmaker of yours?"

"You'll only find out if you can defeat me."

"I was already set on doing such."

The Chaser grabbed Flrange by his watery coat, however, the water demon twirled himself around in the water, causing the Chaser to loosen his grip. Flrange speared the Chaser through the waters, deep until they impacted into the firmament itself. Not a dent. Flrange held the Chaser down with his foot on his throat and laughed.

"It appears your fire cannot conjure within the waters."

The Chaser's eyes quickly opened, only revealing the sinfire. Flrange stumbled as the Chaser shoved his foot from his throat and the Chaser grabbed Flrange by his neck and covered his face with his other hand.

"You've seemed to have forgotten where we are, demon. There are no boundaries here that you can undo."

The Chaser blasted Flrange with sinfire mixed with the waters and evaporated the demon into nothing but remnants of ash. The Chaser took a moment of refreshment before returning to the earth below. Once returning to the earth, the Chaser placed himself in the presence of John and Widow as they were already seeking his presence.

"Good you're here." John said.

"I felt your sense. I came as I could."

"We've discovered something." Widow said.

"Is it of Demonticronto?"

"It is."

Before John could tell the details, Dieheart appeared before them. Applauding with a great smile. Widow hid behind John as he stood next to the Chaser, who's eyes were piercing with fire. And embers brewing from his hands.

"You managed to do it. You took out the demons."

"I did." The Chaser added. "You must be the dealmaker the water spirit spoke of."

"I am. Allow me to introduce myself to you. I am Dieheart. From a realm not of this earth."

"I am aware. The darkness which consumes you is emitting from your very being."

"Of course. I've already introduced myself to John and Widow. When they were seeking answers from a teller."

The Chaser paused, turning to the two.

"You spoke with a fortune teller?"

"We needed a sure answer." Widow responded. "I thought it would be simple."

The Chaser turned to John, who stood quietly. The Chaser waved his hand before turning to Dieheart.

"The deal has been made, Soul of Retribution."

"What deal?"

"You will find out very soon."

Dieheart sunk into the earth with a laugh fading away. The Chaser looked back at John and Widow.

"We'll discuss this later. Right now, get yourselves some time. Mediate. Pray. Prepare yourself for what's ahead."

"What is ahead?" John asked.

"A greater fight."

TRAVIS VAIL, SPIRIT-SEEKER: LOST GIRLS AND FOUND

I

ANOTHER LOST GIRL

Travis Vail sat at his desk, looking over the cases which have been reported ever since the conflicts with Balthazar, the Sin Phantom, and Demonticronto. Vail remembered his encounters with the other supernatural forces. He chuckled under his breath memorizing their allegiance for the moment. He looked over as his cell phone began to vibrate.

"Who's calling?" Vail answered.

Vail listened and he listened closely. He nodded, taking out a pen and writing down the information. He nodded, ending the call. He looked at what he wrote and shook his head.

"Guess it's begun again."

He grabbed his gear, put on his coat and left. Sometime later, Vail arrived in the town where the call had come.

"Back in Chesterfield." Vail sighed. "Let's see what's happening here."

While in Chesterfield, Vail searched for the caller. The caller left an address for Vail to find. Which he traced, finding the address to be in the suburbs. A quiet neighborhood. Vail saw several children playing with each other in a field across the street. Others rode their bikes down the road. Confused, he found the address and approached the home's front door. Vail knocked. The door answered and Vail was surprised.

"Cooper Lawrence?" Vail said.

"Good to see you again, Mr. Vail."

"Wait, you're the one who called?"

"I am."

"But why? What's happened?"

"Come in and we'll explain everything."

"Certainly."

Inside the home, Cooper's wife, Janice saw Vail and she went to greet him. Sitting in the living room was Carrie. Vail saw her and she saw him.

"She's gotten older over the past few years, hasn't she?" Vail said.

"I'm not a child anymore." Carrie said.

"How old are you now? Fifteen? Sixteen?"

"I'm sixteen."

"You're not getting into any trouble, are you?"

"None of a major issue."

"Ah." Vail mumbled."

He turned back to her parents with a concerned, yet unworried look.

"Why did you call me?"

"Please come with us. We'll explain in private."

Vail nodded and followed Carrie's parents into Cooper's office. Once Vail had entered, Cooper closed the door as Vail sat down in front of the desk. Janice sat next to him while Cooper sat behind the desk. Vail was still confused, looking back and forth between Cooper and Janice.

"Why did you call me? I'm not understanding what's happening here."

"We called you because it's starting again." Janice said.

"What's starting again?"

"Carrie's been speaking to someone in her room."

"You're sure it's not just a friend of hers. Perhaps a lad she met at school?"

"No." Cooper said. "That was we thought. Until we overheard her say the name, Leta."

Vail sat back in the chair. Quiet within himself. Leta had returned? Vail was unsure of the possibility.

"Are you sure we're talking about the same Leta? The one who possessed your daughters all those years ago?"

"We're certain." Janice said. "We've never met any of Carrie's friend who have that name."

"You believe Leta is trying to continue what she started?"

"Yes. Why bother our daughter when she's done nothing wrong. She's a good kid."

"That's the thing, Cooper. Good children are often the targets for such spirits."

"So, will you do what you did before?" Janice questioned. "I'm positive it will cleanse her again."

"I will try. But I must be sure of all of this. Carrie's older now and the connection could be deeper than before. I cannot risk anything of importance. Carrie's life depends on it."

"Thank you." Janice replied.

"Please, do what you can." Cooper added.

"I will."

Vail left the home and went to the library, as per usual.

II

<u>REMEMBERING THE ONE BEFORE</u>

Travis Vail sat by himself in the library, reading up on the same files as before. He closed the books and pulled out his phone, dialing a number. On the other end was Raynard Brown. Vail had begun to tell him of Leta's possible return and the connection she has with Carrie Lawrence. Raynard refereed him to search the home's land once more to find anything unusual that may pertain toward the Lost Girl spirit.

"I will do that, Raynard. Just to be sure."

Vail hanged up and left the library, returning to the Lawrence home. While walking back to his car, he saw a homeless man sitting on the sidewalk beside the library. He was cloaked in a black hooded jacket from his shoulders to his knees. He walked with a hunch in his back and frail in his steps. Vail nodded toward him and the man stood up, approaching him. His hands were out and Vail grinned.

"I would give you something if I had anything. I'm sorry."

"Don't be sorry, Spirit-Seeker."

"Pardon?"

The man raised his head up, facing Vail. He stepped back, seeing the homeless man's face. He was old, very old. His long white beard was stretched outward and his eyes were near dim.

"How do you know who I am?" Vail questioned.

"I've been around for a very long time. I've seen those of your kind for many centuries do the work you're doing this day."

"Who are you?"

"I'm only a wanderer, Spirit-Seeker. I come and I go."

"A wanderer? From what part of the world?"

"A place far from here. Across the pond you could say."

"East lands, huh. I see. Well, I need to get going."

"As you shall. For I am aware of the task set before you. The Lost Girl has returned. Hasn't she? Attempting to bond with another host?"

"So I've been told. I'll stop her for good this time."

"I'm sure you will. But, take heed to these words. Her connection with the young girl isn't as simple as you would assume it to believed. For when a spirit goes out of one, it indeed returns much stronger and with friends of its own."

"I know the works. No need to repeat them to me."

"Of course. Now, you will see them in action. Take care, Spirit-Seeker."

Vail nodded, waving away as he turned to his car. He looked back and the man was gone.

"Every time."

III

THE STRANGE CASE OF LETA AND CARRIE

Vail returned to the Lawrence home, seeing Janice running out of the home toward him with Cooper behind.

"What's going on?" Vail asked.

"It's Carrie." Janice said. "There's something wrong with her."

'Wait here. I'll go look to her."

Vail ran into the home, seeing Carrie standing in the living room completely still. Her hair moved smoothly as if the wind was within the home. Vail couldn't feel it as he approached her.

"Carrie, whatever she has on you, you must fight it."

Carrie did not move. Her hands twitched but could not bend. Her fingers were straightened. As if there was electricity holding them in place. Vail took another step forward and Carrie's head turned toward him in a quick rush. Her eyes were solid black, and she grinned. Vail sighed.

"You're not Carrie."

"I am not."

"Leta, release her from your control. Now."

"You believe this will end as it did before? I have learned much since our last encounter."

"I'm sure you have. Still bothering this young girl with your agendas for control."

"We share a bond. A bond that you broke."

"You don't belong here, spirit."

"Your words will not save Carrie this time. I have grown in such spiritual power since the last departure."

"You will leave Carrie and you will be gone for good."

"Make your move. Spirit-Seeker."

Vail reached into his pocket, taking out his book used in many of his cases. He began to recite a page and while doing such, Leta let out a great laugh. The laugh irritated Vail to the point where his reciting had ceased, and he could not utter the words. Vail immediately felt powerless, seeing Leta had truly grown in the spiritual arts. Peculiar for a spirit in Vail's words. Vail had no other options in his place. He paused himself, seeing the black eyes on Carrie and the laughter of Leta coming from her mouth.

"I know." Vail whispered. "I know what I have to do."

Vail placed the book into his jacket pocket, pointed toward Leta while walking back to the door.

"This is far from over."

"Where are you going?!"

"I have something in mind to get rid of you."

"You believe you can cast me away? After what I've just shown you?!"

"Not me. I know a guy and I'll be back with him on my side. And hers."

"I cannot let you leave."

"You will if you let Carrie have control of her body. When I return, then you can rise up and face me. Then, we'll see who will remain."

"Are you challenging me? Using this young girl as a tool for your works?"

"Truth be told, who's the tool in this story? It's not Carrie."

Vail walked back outside, seeing Cooper and Janice waiting in a slight panic mode. Janice ran up to him with tears in her eyes.

"Is she alright?!"

"Unfortunately, Leta has possession over your daughter."

"Aren't you going to do what you did the last time?"

"I tried. Didn't work."

"Then, what are you planning on doing, Mr. Vail?" Cooper asked.

"I know a guy who can help me with this case. Leta's become far stronger than the last time. I'll need some assistance with this one."

Vail walked to his car before turning back to the Lawrences.

"By the way, your daughter should be back to her senses. Leta would have left knowing what I'm planning on doing. Keep an eye on her until I return."

Vail left the Lawrence home. Traveling nearly afar off into the outskirts, stumbling upon an old building. Vail exited his car, approaching the building. The structure was pre-Civil War, yet with a mixture of medieval architecture. Vail nodded.

"This is the spot."

Vail walked up to the large double-doors and knocked. After a second knock, the doors open. Yet, Vail saw no one. He shrugged his shoulders and entered the building with the doors shutting behind him. The closing of the doors did not faze nor concern him. Vail continued walking forward, finding himself standing in a large room near a corridor.

"Hey, I know you're here." Vail said. "So, do us a favor and come on out."

Vail turned around, seeing a large window and hovering at the window was a silhouette of a figure, levitating in the air. Vail smirked, crossing his arms.

"I know who you are." Vail said.

The figure moved forward toward Vail, as he did not move himself. the figure came into the light and revealed itself to be Doctor Donald Fortune. Vail applauded.

"I knew this was your spot all along."

"One of many." Fortune said. "Why are you here, Travis Vail, Spirit-Seeker?"

"You're aware of my work?"

"I know everything that pertains to the mystic realms which surround our world."

"That's nice. Look, I need your help. It's a major concern."

"My help? Why?"

"There's a young girl. She's possessed by a spirit. A powerful spirit. I need your help in breaking the soul tie between them."

"Last I read, you call on the one who's words you read from your book. Didn't you at least try that?"

"I worked last time. Leta's grown more powerful since then."

"Leta." Fortune said. "The Lost Girl spirit."

"Yes. You've heard of her?"

"I've dealt when her kind before. Just not Leta herself."

"She's become stronger after I sent her away. I'm not sure how."

"You're telling me you were the one who sent her away those years ago?"

"I am. I was younger and much of a novice in those days. But, I did what needed to be done to save the girl."

"Now, Leta's retuned to the same girl and has an even stronger hold on her?"

"That's correct."

"I understand."

Fortune opened the doors of the building to the outside. Vail looked back and forth to the door and to Fortune.

"Aren't you going to tell me what to do? I need to break the soul tie between them."

"Yes, you do." Fortune replied. "However, I will not allow you to go alone."

"Why can't you just tell me what to do? I can deal with Leta myself."

"I need to see this Leta in person. Learn her motives. That way, I can prepare myself and my apprentice in case she returns again in the future."

"Your apprentice? There's no one else here."

"He's preoccupied on a task afar off. Now, are you ready to save this girl?"

"After you."

"I'll meet you there."

"Wait a second, fellow. You don't even know where she is."

"I'll follow your lead. You drove out here after all. You can drive back."

"Can't you just teleport us there. And the car?"

"I can. But, should I?"

"It would prove much faster and speed is what we'll need to get rid of Leta."

"Very true. Stand still."

"Ok. Why-"

IV

A STUBBORN SPIRIT ENTERS THE PIT

Within a sudden moment, Vail and Fortune were standing in front of the Lawrence home. Vail looked around, seeing the home and even his car. He turned to Fortune, who only nodded.

"How'd you do that?"

"The Orb of Quirinto." Fortune answered, showing the org attached to the amulet around his neck. Glowing with mystical energy.

"Where did you get it?"

"A long story not worth telling at the moment. We need to get Leta out of the girl."

"Agreed."

"I'm assuming she's inside." Fortune said.

"Let's go in then."

They approached the door of the home with Janice opening it as soon as she saw Vail. Cooper ran up behind her, confused about Fortune's appearance.

"Mr. Vail, who's the friend?"

"He's going to help me save your daughter."

"Who is he supposed to be?" Janice asked. "Some kind of magician."

"Sorcerer, madam."

"We assumed Vail could handle this on his own." Cooper mentioned. "Like the last time."

"This isn't like the last time." Vail replied. "Leta has a much stronger hold on Carrie. Doctor Fortune is here to aid me in setting your daughter free."

"Is your friend capable of this kind of work?"

"I've faced much more and far worse than a possession. I'm skilled enough."

Cooper nodded, allowing Fortune to enter the home. Upon entering, Fortune saw Carrie's body levitating above the living room floor. Vail entered, seeing the levitation.

"She's getting stronger."

"We have this under control." Fortune said. "I desire to speak with Leta."

Carrie's body moved around in the air as her head turned toward Fortune's gaze and her eyes were locked on. Still black. She grinned heavily, starting Carrie's parents.

"Vail, you've returned. And I see you didn't come alone."

"I did not."

Fortune stepped forward as a gust of wind rustled from Carrie's body, shoving him and Vail back. Fortune twirled his arms and the wind ceased. Vail noticed the tactic and shrugged his shoulders.

"That's convenient."

"Who are you?" Leta's voice asked.

"I am Doctor Donald Fortune. Supreme Enchanter of the mystical realm and I have been brought here to rid you of this young girl and of this material world."

"Supreme Enchanter? Another one?"

"She's familiar with your kind." Vail noticed. "Are you sure you can handle this, Fortune?"

"I am positive." Fortune clapped his hands together with the energy covering them. "Prepare to do your part in this, Spirit-Seeker."

"My part?"

"Do what you've done before. I will handle the rest."

Vail turned to Carrie's parents. Telling them to go outside and wait until the work is done. They agreed with tears in their eyes as the left the house. Vail turned his focus back toward Leta, while Fortune began levitating just a few feet off the ground. Leta had full control over Carrie's body, now posing it against Fortune. Vail slowly reached into his pocket, grabbing his book.

"Do you have what you need?" Fortune asked.

45

"I do."

"Then you're ready."

"I am."

Leta rushed toward Fortune as he stretched forth his arms, creating a barrier between himself and Leta. Vail was in the middle of the barrier with his book opened. Fortune looked toward him and nodded. Vail started to recite from the book the same words as before. Leta's focus was not on Vail, but on Fortune as she tried beating down the mystic barrier. She screamed with rage, punching the barrier. Fortune kept his demeanor. Focused and in control as Vail continued reading.

"Add one more to the speech." Fortune told Vail. "And speak it in something other than Latin."

"I got it." Vail replied. "*Tam qate alhabl alfidiya baynak wabaynaha alan!*"

Leta turned to Vail as he closed the book. Her eyes began to show the pupils as she struggled to hold herself and Carrie together. Her body was fighting between staying levitated and coming down to the floor. She glared toward Fortune as he could see Carrie's eyes starting to appear and Leta's power decreasing.

"You heard him, Lost Girl. The soul tie is broken. Leave. Now."

Fortune clapped his hands and the barrier collapsed as Leta let out a great scream. Carrie's body floated and fell to the floor, not before Vail could catch her. Fortune cleared the home of any residue of Leta's power. About thirty minutes later, Carrie's parents entered the home to find Carrie laying down in her room on the bed.

"Is she alright?" Janice asked.

"She's well." Vail said. "Leta is gone."

"Oh. Thank you. Thank you both."

Fortune nodded. Cooper approached the two and shook their hands. Thanking them for their help. Vail wanted to wait for Carrie to wake up and once she did, he spoke to her with Fortune standing by. Carrie told Vail that she was aware of everything that was happening. She stated she no longer feels the connection she shared with Leta. But, she told him that she could also see Leta's intentions. Her intentions were dire, and she was brought forth by a sorcerer who saw fit to distract Vail from some grander plan.

"Don't concern yourself with our affairs." Vail said. "We're just glad you're alright."

Afterwards, Vail said his goodbyes, hoping he doesn't have to return due to such similar events. Later, Vail spoke with Fortune about Carrie's words and he understood them greatly. Fortune warned Vail about an opposing adversary of his to which Vail stated he had no adversaries. Balthazar could be counted as one, but not a great adversary.

"I'm referring to anyone you met in your early years." Fortune said. "Someone who was very peculiar to your work. Like an opposite of the coin."

Vail thought, "There was one, however I haven't seen him since the investigation."

"I see. Meanwhile, you should keep an eye out. Just in case."

"One more thing." Vail said. "Why did you tell me not to speak the words in Latin?"

"Because you have to get outside of your box when confronting these matters. Spirits such as Leta keep memories, you know."

"Informative of you."

"Arabic was an interesting choice."

"It's the first one that came to mind."

"Good to hear. Just keep watch. All that Carrie told you, do not forget it."

"I will keep it all in mind. Thank you for the assistance, Doctor."

"It was a necessary duty."

Fortune warped the surroundings into a portal back to his true residence, the Citadel of Enchantment. Vail saw the large structure and how it was placed amongst the trees in a wilderness afar off. Vail smirked.

"That's where you reside."

"Indeed. I will be seeing you around, Travis Vail."

"Until next time."

"We'll see, Spirit-Seeker."

Fortune entered the portal and was gone. Vail took in the moment before entering his car and driving away, mediating on all that transpired. While on the road, Vail accepted the though in his heart and mind that Leta was gone. For good this time. To him, it was a great victory for the living.

THE DEVIL HUNTER: BLOODLUST GROUNDS

I

ANOTHER AMBUSH?

Once he returned to Washington D.C., Gabriel Abraham went about his business. His first duty was to track down Sierra the Succubus, whom had escaped in the woods during the battle with Hastur's demons. Abraham returned to the same forest as before, except without the assistance of Evan Wyatt or Andrea Coralline. He searched the area of the last encounter with Sierra and found nothing but dried bones of her victims. Abraham shook his head.

"Where could she be?"

Behind Abraham appeared seven shrouded figures. Cloaked in dark robes. Their faces were hidden by the hoods. Abraham turned toward them, pointing at their apparel and he scoffed loudly.

"You guys again? I thought the whole incident at the church was a clear message."

"We are not with the Cult." One of the shrouded ones said.

"Then enlighten me on who's your with. If you're with anyone to be mentioned."

"We want you to know our master knows of your works. He seeks to find you and to bring you in."

"Your master? I have to guess. It can't be Hastur because we already dealt with him. Is it Demonticronto? No? How about the Sin Phantom? Not him either. Well, you're have to do some talking with me to get my mind cleared."

"No need. Once our master gets an audience with you, he will clear your mind of all things you deeply desire. You will only desire his power and his will alone."

"And you said you're not with the Cult? Yet, you're talking the same message with me right now. They said about the same."

"Our master is very powerful."

"And your master has been around for centuries. It's no different than the others. Now, I will ask you simply to leave me be while I do my work. Otherwise, prepare yourselves for a fight."

The shrouded ones lunged toward Abraham with fangs. He saw the teeth immediately and slammed his hands into the ground. The earth quaked and opened beneath them, swallowing the shrouded ones. Before the last one was taken down into the pit, it glared at Abraham.

"Our master will find out what you've done and he will find you. Sooner than the sun can touch this city on the morning!"

The shrouded one fell into the pit and the hole was sealed. Silence covered the grounds and Abraham turned back to the bones. Still no sign of Sierra. Abraham brushed off his shoulders and entered his car, leaving the area to return to the Revelation Center.

II

HUNTINGS

Abraham enter the Center, finding Evan and Andrea scrambling in the library. Grabbing books which pertained to the recent events with Demonticronto. Evan and Andrea were somewhat jealous of Abraham's team-up with Travis Vail and the others. Abraham chuckled from their words and only waved his hands as he walked toward his office.

"There's something else going on. The reading can pause for a moment."

They entered his office as he grabbed a book from the shelf and opened it. On the pages were the same shrouded figures he encountered in the wilderness. He began telling them about their matching descriptions and how they proclaimed themselves not part of Hastur's Cult. Evan quickly assumed they were due to the similarities of appearance. Andrea was a little curious as to who they worship. If not Hastur, then who?

"I'm not sure." Abraham said. "But, one of them told me their master will find me before the sun rises. We only have about six hours till then."

"Well, what do you want us to do?" Evan asked. "Seal up the doors and windows?"

"This won't end up like last time. Whoever their master is, they talked well of him. So, I'm not expecting an ambush. Besides, they said he wishes to bring me into his group."

"Bring you in?" Andrea asked. "That would mean he's already aware of your existence and who you are."

"All I ask is that we be ready for his arrival. With only six hours till sunrise, he'll be here much sooner than we'll be expecting."

Evan crest his chin while looking at the images of the shrouded ones.

He pointed in the air and clapped his hands. Abraham and Andrea turned toward him in confusion. Abraham stared at him.

"Looking for some music to play?"

"No. I just thought of something. The words listed here, they describe these figures of having sharp fangs and using them to attack their victims. All of this sounds like they're some group of-"

"Vampires." Abraham replied. "I know. I saw the fangs myself before they went deep into the pit."

"Wait." Andrea paused. "First, we had to deal with some great demon. Then, you go off on an adventure with the Spirit-Seeker, then you have a team-up with a bunch of supernatural entities to fight against a demon stronger than Hastur. Now, you're telling us that vampires are around? Have been around?"

"You didn't know?" Abraham questioned.

"I just wasn't certain they existed."

"Much like werewolves, demons, ghosts, and superheroes, yeah. Vampires exist. In different forms as well. The movies don't usually get them correct most of the time."

"Well, Andrea." Evan said. "Now you know."

Andrea shook her head and left Abraham's office. Evan followed her out while Abraham grinned. He grabbed the book and looked at the images himself. Turning the pages, he began to learn a little of their master. An ancient entity. Their master made them into what they became. They live to worship and obey him only. Abraham was intrigued by this figure and graciously waited for the entity to show up at the Center. Abraham was not going anywhere nor was he planning on hiding.

In an abandoned ghost town. Deep underneath the town itself was the remnants of a medieval catacombs. The catacombs was damp, with tiny rivers of water flowing through and throughout. However, there was a heat coming from within the catacombs. A peculiar heat. Inside, there was a solid black coffin. Made of onyx and heated in a great temperature. The coffin's lid tilted and slid open. Out of the coffin came a hand, pale with white fingernails. The smell of sulfur irradiated from within the coffin as the figure stood up on the outside. Cloaked in all black. He raised his head up to the sky and sniffed.

"Ah." He uttered quietly. "Devilhunter."

III

MEET THE MASTER

With almost an hour till sunrise and still no sign of the shrouded ones' master. Evan waited in the lobby with a sword in hand. Abraham walked out of his office, seeing Evan with the sword and shook his head.

"Put that down. No need to hurt yourself before the enemy approaches."

Evan put down the sword, sitting it next to the wall near the bookshelf. Andrea entered the library, seeing Abraham standing with Evan. She closed the book in her hands.

"What did Evan do this time?"

"What?" Evan said.

"Nothing. He was just practicing his swordsmanship."

They laughed and the sound of the front door creaked into the library. They looked at one another and immediacy went to see who had entered. Evan stood up and before he left the library, he grabbed the sword. They entered the lobby and saw who had enter the Center. He was dressed in all black. A long robe with a cloak. Yet, no hood. His skin was pale and his beard was dark as a raven. His eyes were red as a fire.

"Well, this guy's not human." Andrea said.

"No kidding." Evan replied.

"I think I know who he is." Abraham said. "It all fits."

"Then, you know why I've come, Devilhunter."

"You're their master. They never told me your name."

"I am aware of what you have done to my followers. Sending them into such a pit where hey will have a hard time returning to the grounds of the earth. No matter. I will seek out new followers and they will

54

worship me. With your help."

Abraham scoffed.

"I'm not helping a vampire achieve anything."

"I am not just a vampire. I am the Head of the Vampires."

"Yeah right." Andrea said. "So, you've been around before Dracula?"

"He is of another matter. I have led the vampire species throughout the eons of our time. I will continue to lead them until the end of all things is at hand."

"Well, the end isn't here yet." Abraham said. "So, here's the deal. You can leave this Center and go back to wherever you've came from. Or you can meet our end this day by my hands."

"And mine." Evan added. "I'm sorry, I just had to get involved."

"I have no desire to fight you, Devilhunter. I know of your works in this field. Your allegiance with the Spirit-Seeker and those others you've met on your quest against the great demon. Fighting you would serve no purpose in the higher affairs."

"Then, why have you come to my place? Last I was told by one of your worshippers that you seek to recruit me into your little cult."

"Only because of what you've accomplished in such a short time. You've built this Center to protect the lives of the innocents. Except for the one you lost some time ago. What if I told you she is still alive."

Abraham paused.

"What are you saying? She's still alive? Where?"

"I cannot give you more information unless you follow me."

The master extended his hand toward Abraham. Andrea and Evan yelled toward him to refuse and step back. Abraham was torn. He knew the Vampire was the enemy, but the thought of finding his lost student gave him such higher cause for his works. Abraham stepped forward and extended his hand toward the vampire. Andrea rushed and the master grabbed her by the throat. Evan raised his sword and swiped the vampire's back. It had no effect as the vampire knocked him across the lobby floor. Abraham held the vampire's hand and he laughed. Abraham smirked with his left hand behind his back, holding a silver dagger.

"I refuse." Abraham said, raising the dagger and stabbing the vampire in the chest.

The master stumbled as he pulled the dagger from his chest, burning his hand in the process. He tossed the dagger to the ground, holding his chest in burning pain. The vampire opened the front doors as he backed up, he looked up to the clouds and piercing through them was sunlight. He snarled.

"I could've given you such power, Devilhunter. Such drive. Such motivation. You could've seen your student again."

"If she is still alive, I'll find another way to save her. As for helping your kind, I refuse."

The Vampire transformed himself into a swarm of bats and left the Center. Abraham shut the doors and sighed. Evan stood up from the floor, grabbing the sword. Andrea approached him, telling him to put it down. Abraham stood quiet while Evan returned to the library.

"You're alright?" Andrea asked.

"I'll be fine."

"His words didn't sink deep, did they?"

"Not deep enough. But, I do wonder if my student is alive. In some other dimension or world. I must know if it is true. Get this burden off my chest."

"Then, what will you do?"

"I'll make a call. See what Vail knows."

"And what if he doesn't?"

"Guess I'll have to wait and see what comes next."

As they talked, a strange figure entered the library, cloaked in a mist of darkness, reached over to the shelves, stealing several books on the occult. The figure hears Evan's footsteps approaching and disappeared through a rift between the worlds.

THE MAN CALLED FABLE:
THE ART OF THE DEAL

I

LET'S HAVE A CHAT

Denise Kira stepped through the doors of the bar. The bar filled with all sorts of magical creatures. Inside, she glanced around at the trolls, satyrs, goblins, elves, and other kinds. She approached the bar as the bartender turned around to see her. Sitting her bag on the top of the bar.

"You're not one of us." The bartender said.

"I'm not. I've come to see someone."

"Someone? Like a lover or something?"

"More like an acutance."

"Ah. Why would they tell you to meet them here? Humans aren't usually visitors to such a place."

"His name is Fable. That's what I was told."

The bartender stopped what he was doing. Only to stare. Denise looked at him, waiting for a word to come out of his mouth.

"You mean to meet with him? The troublemaker?"

"Troublemaker? He helped me."

"Listen closely. Fable is a guy who comes and goes. He never stays. Unless there's a price willing to be paid."

"Must be a large sum." A voice said from around the bar.

They turned to see Fable, leaning against the bar with a smirk on his face. The bartender sighed. Denise smiled. Fable smiled back before looking at the bartender with a questionable face.

"Tell me, what have you told the woman?"

"Only that you're trouble. You'll always be trouble with the path you're on."

"Trouble can go a lot of ways. Good or bad. Best to take our chances."

"Hmm." The bartender turned and went about his business.

Fable nodded toward Denise.

"I see you came."

"Well, you told me to meet you here. Figured you would show up again."

"And I did. Although, not to drink and gamble as before. you wanted to talk, so we'll talk."

Denise agreed and the two went to a table near one of the windows at the back of the bar. Fable preferred such an area. Gives him a full view of the place and all who are inside can be seen by him. His eyes were focused just as his revolver was loaded. The bartender came to their table, setting down a mug. Fable grabbed the mug.

"Thanks."

"I'm doing it for the woman. Not for you."

"No offense taken." Fable grinned.

The bartender walked away as Fable took a drink from the mug. He sighed as Denise watched on.

"So, what did you want to talk about?"

"Um, what had happened in town. Between you and the other guy."

"Oh. You speak of Emblem. He's a troublesome lad. Never met him until that very moment."

"And what of the woman? The hooded one."

"Pandora. She's a nice girl. Although, she can be trouble at times. Drives me insane."

"Well, she visited me at my apartment."

"When?"

"Before I saw you on the streets with her and Emblem. She warned me not to be around you. Said you were trouble. Damnation would occur."

"Damnation? Ha. Pandora does have the soft spot for those words. I wouldn't mind her sayings. She's an ancient individual."

"She told me the world has enough to deal with. Due to the risen heroes."

"Ah, those peeps. Listen, Denise, I've never encountered any of them. Do I wish to meet some? Perhaps one day. Until then, I do what I can for Manchester."

"There is something I would like to know."

"Shoot for it."

"Have you ever crossed over through the Rift?"

"I have. When I was a young lad."

"What is it like? The place?"

"Very… magical." Fable grinned.

"I'm sure it is. Are the colors brighter there than they are here?"

"Much brighter. If the general public saw what was beyond the Rift, they would believe they're in an alien's world."

"And those who live there?"

"Very magical. Trolls, elves, dwarves. All types of races."

"Do they get along?"

"It's more complicated to explain. But, they have their methods."

"I'm sorry to keep digging, but there must be a lot more."

"There is. And if I were to tell you, we would be in this bar for days. That is time we cannot toss away. Give it some time and eventually, you will come to know it all. Eventually."

"I see."

"Don't worry yourself. It will come. In time."

"I'm sure of it."

"Oh. By the way. You don't need to call me Fable. Let the blokes do that."

"Then, what shall I call you?"

"Kurt. Kurt Wesker."

"Very well. Kurt."

Denise smiled as Fable continued to drink.

In a far-off location within the Rift, Pandora stood before The Hidden Four. Surrounded by fire, crystals sticking out the walls with various gemstones. Magic filled the place. It had a presence of its own.

The Four aren't pleased with the previous actions of Fable when contending with Emblem. Pandora had sought out to reason for him before the Four, as they seek to pull him from the duty of the task.

"Fable is a skilled ally. When necessary."

"Necessary is not the focus on the task." One of the Four spoke. "We see that he should take these mattes urgently and complete them."

"I will send word to him about your concerns. I cannot change his mind."

"But, you can speak with him. See what it will take to get him on these matters. Quickly. Emblem is not far away. He is healing himself as we speak and he craves revenge."

"I can feel him." Pandora said. "Although, I shall be ready for the fight."

"And you will make sure Fable is ready as well."

"That I will." Pandora sighed before vanishing in a whiff of reddish smoke.

II

<u>NICE TO MEET YOU</u>

After the conversation in the bar, Denise and Fable returned to their homes. When Denise had arrived and turned on the lights, Pandora was standing before her. The presence of the hooded one startled Denise as she dropped her books and bag. She knelt to pick them up, however Pandora raised her hand and the objects lifted from the floor and onto the table near the kitchen. Denise nodded.

"I appreciate that."

"I must speak with you." Pandora said. "It is of urgent matters."

"You're not going to mute me again are you?"

"Only if you make such a loud sound."

"I won't. Why are you in my apartment? Again?"

"To speak to you, of course."

"Why me? I haven't done nothing wrong."

"You did not heed my warnings about Fable."

"He seems like a decent man."

"He is dangerous. The things that follow him only bring tragedy to those outside of the magic realm."

"He told me enough about the Rift and how it operates."

Pandora paused herself.

"What do you mean? he spoke more of the magic?"

"Yes. It was just him and I. nothing else. I asked some questions, he gave me answers."

"Where is he now?" Pandora asked.

"He said he was heading home."

61

"Very well. I will speak to him as soon as possible. For the meantime, anything he has told you, keep it to yourself. Do not speak of this to another human."

"And if I end up doing so?"

"Do not make me find you. Or anyone else from the magic realm."

Denise nodded with a slight pause.

"I see."

"I am positive we will meet again."

"I'm sure of it." Denise replied.

Pandora snapped her fingers and she vanished. Denise sighed.

Fable had returned to the Cheshire Plain. Sitting in his home peacefully. Until he moment a tremor occurred. He arose from his seat, his left-hand glowing with magical energy while his right hand is placed on his revolver. The shaking of the land increased, traveling toward Fable's home. He placed himself, ready to fight as the front door opened. Revealing the Hidden Four.

"Really?" Fable sighed. "Again?"

The Four entered the home as the door shut behind them. They surrounded Fable.

"What's going on here?"

"We are here to insure you of your duties."

"What duties?"

"Your duties to stopping Emblem."

"Yeah. Emblem. I remember the lad. Pandora and I faced him in town. We defeated him and he ran away."

"He did leave the area. Yes. However, he has retreated to heal himself and to grow stronger."

"So I've been told."

"When he does make his presence known, you must be there to eliminate him."

"I see. And what of Pandora? Will she be accompanying me on this quest?"

"Pandora will do what she is commanded to do."

Fable nodded with a slight scoff.

"I'm sure she will. By the way, where is she?"

"She is on matters which attend to the quest at hand."

"Ah. So, she's going about the realms. Back and forth."

"You must accompany her on this next task."

"What task? I've already said I'll help against Emblem."

"This concerns another. Another powerful force. You and Pandora will travel into the Rift. There, you will meet with Chernabog."

Fable coughed.

"Pardon. Chernabog?"

"Chernabog has some information concerning Emblem that will be valuable for you and Pandora to learn. See to it that you visit him. There is much to be done at such a short time."

"And we are supposed to trust him?"

"You will do what is necessary. That is all."

The Four turned from Fable and left his home in a collected fashion. Fable only took a sip of his drink and shook his head.

"Every time."

III

<u>CHERNABOG</u>

Fable had met up with Pandora at the Gate of the Rift. There, Pandora had told him of her meeting with Denise, to which Fable could only wondered of what reason. Pandora stated she told Denise to stay away from him and Fable disagreed. He understood her reasons, but he saw himself as no consequence or threat to Denise's life. Pandora shook her head hearing the words coming from Fable.

"Let's just speak to Chernabog and get this over with." Fable said.

"Finally." Pandora chuckled. "You're focus on important matters."

Fable scoffed at Pandora's words as they walked through the gate and into the Rift. Once through, they found themselves standing at the doorway to what seemed to be an abandoned shack. Pandora looked around the shack, seeing no entry points besides the front door. Fable pointed toward it as Pandora continued searching.

"We could just knock." Fable suggested.

"I'm not certain we should. Chernabog is one not to be easily missed."

"We won't miss him if we just knock."

Fable went ahead and knocked. There was no response. Fable knocked once again, still no answer. Fable sighed and knocked three times before kicking the door once.

"What was that for?" Pandora asked.

"To get a response. The knocks weren't doing good."

As they were speaking, the door creaked open with the sound of a whistling wind. The air pulled out with the door, causing Fable and Pandora to question where they stand. Within the doorway was only a long hall. Deep down into a path of darkness. Pandora took a step forward and a strange odor moved across her face. She frowned, shaking her head.

"What is it?" Fable wondered.

"The stench. Blood."

They proceeded to enter the shack. Walking down the hallway led them into a larger room. One that would seem impossible to dwell within a shack such as the one they saw on the outside. Fable realized it is all an illusion, just as many places within the Rift are. Sitting inside the room was a man, one who had the similitude of an elder. His long white and black beard flowed down to his chest. His long black hair sat over his shoulders. Above his head he wore a silver crown. His eyes were dark as the night, yet glowing as the red of fire. He was dressed in armor resembling the Middle Age.

"Is this him?" Fable asked, staring at him.

Pandora stood before him as his eyes raised up toward hers. He grinned.

"Chernabog. I am Pandora. This is Fable. We are here on urgent matters concerning Emblem."

"I know of you." Chernabog replied, standing up from the chair. "I am aware of all that has transpired."

"You do?" Fable said. "How?"

"I have my followers throughout the natural realm."

"Then, you know all there is about Emblem?"

"I do. You want him destroyed? Yes?"

"We want him stopped." Pandora stated.

"I just want him gone." Fable said. "Guy's becoming an annoyance."

"Hmm. Well, those hoods told you all there is to know. You came to me as was scheduled. Now, I must deliver to you what you've come for."

"And that is?" Pandora questioned.

"You will need me to help you defeat Emblem. But, I do not rise up and fight for a cause unless one of my own is finished."

"What are you on about?" Fable said. "What cause?"

"I will lend my power to the battle if the two of you eliminate an ally of Emblem and an enemy of mine."

"And who is this enemy?"

"He calls himself Dark Fright. A frightening figure to humanity. Appears as a human/bat hybrid. He is very skilled. Born in the Rift like many of us, but his power comes from a darker source. Shit, even darker than my own."

"Listen, we are not hear to do your errands." Pandora stated. "We are here to get your assistance."

"You will have my assistance when you take out Dark Fright." Chernabog replied calmly. "Now, do you want my help or not?"

Pandora grunted, staring at Chernabog while Fable stepped forward, with his hands clapped together.

"Panny, we need his help."

"Panny?" Chernabog noticed. "Is that what he calls you? And you allow it?"

"That is not my name and he knows it."

"He wants to agree. I agree."

"Look, we can go on out there, find this Fright fellow and take him out. That way, Chernabog here can help us defeat Emblem."

"I know, Fable. I know." Pandora shook herself. "Fine, we will confront Dark Fright. Then, you will aid us."

"I will. You have my word and my bond."

"Your word is received. Your bond is not."

Pandora turned away from Chernabog while Fable looked back at the Slavic god. Chernabog nodded and Fable walked away, following Pandora out of the shack.

Within the realm of the Rift, Emblem sat in a throne room made of gold and iron. In the throne's seat, Emblem sat still, his wounds from the fight with Fable and Pandora continue to heal as his body is made whole. Emblem let out a small breath as he heard footsteps entering the room.

"Who's here?"

"I am, my lord."

Emblem raised his head to see Dark Fright standing before him. The man/bat hybrid entity clothed in dark-clad armor with a helmet resembling medieval knights with two wings on each side. His armor appeared to look black, but in the sunlight of the Rift, it shined a violet hue. Dark Fright was on one knee before Emblem.

"Rise." Emblem said.

"I heard you needed my services."

"I do. There are two who seek to take me out. They wounded me a bit in our last encounter. I have summoned you to face them and eliminate them. By any means."

"May I ask who they are?"

"Pandora, the hooded woman and The Man Called Fable."

"Pandora is still doing the Cloaks' bidding?"

"She is and she has a human on her side. But, he's very keen of our world and the magic powers that exists. He's seen out world with his own eyes. Keep your eyes on him, he is a sneaky one. Clever in his tricks and powerful in the arts."

"I will complete this task, my lord." Fright bowed before leaving the throne room.

IV

<u>SEAL THE TAKE</u>

Fable and Pandora exited the Rift, returning to Manchester. Finding themselves at the front of the bar where Fable attends, they see a figure staring at them. Fable noticed the helmet and quickly pulled out his revolver and fired a shot. The figure dodged the round by disappearing in a flash of black smoke. Pandora noticed the sound, turning toward the smoke.

"What was that?" Fable asked.

"The one Chernabog told us to find."

The smoke gathered itself and formed Dark Fright in front of them. Fright groaned as he faced off with Fable and Pandora. Fable went for another shot, but Fright caught the round in his hand, crushing it into ash as it fell from his hand. Fable squinted.

"Damn."

"You know why we must take you down." Pandora said.

"You said the name Chernabog. That tells me all I must know."

"You are in our path against Emblem. I will not let that stand."

"You have no say in the matters!"

"Look." Fable gestured. "Can we just get this over with?"

"I agree with this one." Fright replied.

Pandora bolted toward Fright with energy blasts. Each one missing the mark as Fright transformed them into the black smoke. From there, Fable went ahead shooting more rounds toward Fright as he blocked the rounds from impact while fighting against Pandora's blasts. Fright speared Pandora to the ground and kicked Fable into the bar wall.

"Enough of this little play." Fright said, clapping his hands as bats emerged from the sky.

"Did he just summon bats?" Fable said. "Like real bats?"

Pandora looked up toward the swarm and rushed toward it, attacking the savage bats with her blasts. Meanwhile, Fable stood up and rushed toward Fright, trying to attack him with punches. Fright's speed was beyond average as he dodged every incoming blow. Fright ducked under the punch, grabbing Fable by the collar of his duster, slamming him into the concrete. Fright turned around, kicking Fable across the ground.

"Shit." Fable grunted. "This guy's strong."

"You are a nuisance, magician."

"I've been told."

Fright walked over to fable, snatching him up by the coat and tossing him into the nearby truck which was parked at the front of the bar. Fable struggled to get up as Pandora appeared from behind Fright, grabbing him by his head, tossing him across the street into the incoming traffic. Fright saw the scenery as an opportunity, rushing into the streets as the vehicles begin to cease and crash. Pandora ran into the street, shoving Fright out of the vehicles' path. Fright laughed.

"Knew you had a soft touch for humanity."

Fright head butted Pandora, backing her into the street as a car rammed her down the road. Fright nodded and walked through the traffic toward Fable at the bar. Fable was on his feet and he looked around for Pandora, not seeing her. He turned forward to see Fright approaching him. He continued firing more shots, but Fright walked through them as the rounds evaporated into smoke once again. Fable sighed.

"It's not enough,"

"You are right, magician. It is not enough."

Fright grabbed Fable by his throat, lifting him off his feet. Fright savored the moment, squeezing Fable's neck.

"I have something to tell you." Fable coughed.

"And that is?"

"You like fairies?"

"What?"

"Do you like fairies?"

"I will not partake in these foolish games!"

"You just have." Fable grinned, opening his hand as dozens of small fairies appeared.

The fairies swarmed al around Fright as he tried swiping them from his body. The fairies covered Fright in their dust, which shined with the sunlight. Fright yelled as the sunlight began piercing through his armor. Fable took notice and fired one more shot at Fright's helmet. The shot blew a hole through Fright's helmet and he fell to the ground. The fairies vanished into a small pocket of the Rift, which opened by Fable's hand. He sealed it as Pandora returned, holding her ribs.

"I see you came back."

"Don't. Do not joke now."

"If not now, when?"

Pandora walked over to Fright's body, seeing the round's entry spot on the helmet. However, she could sense Fright was not dead, just unconscious. Fable sighed as he approached her, looking down at Fright. Fable nodded.

"So, we've completed the task. We've defeated Dark Fright."

"Indeed you have." a voice said from behind them.

They turned to see Chernabog exiting the bar with a drink in his hand.

"You were in there the whole time?" Fable asked,

"Well, yes. I had to keep close eyes on you. Only to make sure you went through with the task. I now see you have."

Chernabog walked over toward them, gazing down at Fright's body. Chernabog grinned and waved his hand, causing fright to vanish. Pandora looked around for Fright, not seeing him. Fable was confused, extending his arms out.

"The hell just happened?"

"What did you do with him?" Pandora questioned. "Where is he?"

"He's right where I want him to be. No need for you or your hooded friends to worry about."

"So, you'll help us with Emblem?"

"You have my support." Chernabog replied, turning away. "You will see me again when the battle commences."

70

"How will we contact you?" Fable asked.

"You won't need to." Chernabog took a last gulp of the drink and disappeared in a dark portal, returning to his shack.

"Well, what do we do now?"

"Return to your home, Fable. I will contact you when the next objective is at hand."

"You or the Hidden Four?"

"I'll do the talking next time."

Sometime later, Fable returned to his home, speaking with Denise over the phone for some hours. Many hours later, a knock came from his door and he went and answered. It was Pandora, breathing heavily.

"What's wrong?"

"The books." Pandora said. "They've been stolen."

"What books?"

"The books. The grimoires of great power."

"Where are they now?"

"I do not know. But, you must find them. You're the only one who can."

"What about you?"

"I have some matters to attend to in the Rift. I will speak to you again soon."

Pandora left his home. Fable shut the door and sighed.

"Back at it again."

CINDERELLA: A HUNTSMAN IN LONDON

I

LONDON CALLING

The City of London have now heard the rumors of Cinderella throughout the area. Civilians arrived out of nowhere, claiming they have seen her at one time or another during the nights. Now, Stepmother Anne had sent out a notice to the city concerning Cinderella's threat to the people. She had hired a Huntsman to track down and find her before she makes a reappearance within the city.

While the city goes in a frenzy concerning the Sly Detective, a fellow woman from Germany arrived at the police headquarters in London. An officer approached her with caution.

"Ma'am." The officer said.

"I have a reason for being here."

"Your name?"

"Snow White."

Snow White later appeared to the people of London, proclaiming herself as a detective who's heard of the Cinderella sightings. Snow believed Cinderella is a product of the risen heroes throughout the world, something she distains. Now, she sees capturing Cinderella as an opportunity of stopping them one at a time.

During the scuffles of the public and the authorities, Cindy sat inside her home with her friend Charlotte, watching the news, seeing the outcry for her arrest. Charlotte shook her head.

"Can't believe they see you as a threat."

"It was bound to happen." Cindy said. "You help them and they want you dead."

"It must be a burden."

"Not exactly. I've done what I can to protect the innocent in this city. Not everyone will see my actions as beneficial."

"What you do is beneficial. To me. To all of us. The things you told me about what you had to do when fighting that demon guy, if these people heard that story, they would appreciate all you have done so far. You helped save the lives of everyone. Not just in London, but the world."

"You know these people don't believe in demons, right." Cindy scoffed.

"But, they seem to believe you exist. Without ever seeing you. Only going by the notions of some bystanders on street corners."

Cindy sighed, laying back on the couch.

"What of your stepmother and sisters?" Charlotte noted. "Have you heard from them about any of this?"

"I know they're behind it. They always are."

"Well, since you're friends with others in your field of expertise, perhaps you could call one of them to help you out with all this."

"I think they're busy enough with their own affairs."

Elsewhere, Stepmother Anne arrived at an office building not too far from Blackpool. She entered and inside the room stood a man. Tall, lean, wielding an axe. Anne paused when she saw him as the guards inside pointed her to the man.

"So, this is the guy." Anne said. "He has the appearance of a hunter."

"You sent word for my skill set." The man said. "I am here to accept your offer."

"This is good. Now, you received all the details to this task?"

"I read you wanted me to find Cinderella. Not sure why you would have me go and search for a fairy tale figure."

"She is not a fairy tale. Not in London anyway."

"Then, who is going around proclaiming themselves to be Cinderella? And why do you wish them captured?"

"Because. She is my stepdaughter. Her actions have led her down this path and I cannot tolerate it any longer. She must be stopped. By any means. She's a capable fighter."

"A fighter? A young woman called Cinderella?"

"She's taken out armies of guards with her own hands. She was trained by a skilled fighter."

"I see. Very well, I will go to London and find your stepdaughter."

"Thank you for your aid in this cause."

II

<u>SCOUTED</u>

Later that night, Cinderella was out, scouting on the trail of her stepmother's criminal affairs. While on the search, the Huntsman was also out searching for Cinderella. After following the path she previously had taken, she returned to the warehouse where she saw her stepmother. There, she entered the building and immediately the alarms went off. Several armed guards rushed out from the doors, aiming their firearms toward her. Cinderella stood still, exhaling slowly.

"Nowhere to run, thief!"

"I'm not running anywhere." Cinderella replied.

"Don't shoot unless she moves first." Another armed man said.

"If I move first? Sure thing."

Cinderella slowly reached in her outer coat pocket as an armed one spotted her arms. He raised his weapon and she tossed out smoke bombs and quickly moved out of their sights as they began firing. She stood over them in the warehouse as the smoke cleared. The men moved with haste searching for her. Some spoke of her stepmother, saying she won't be happy with her reappearance.

Over at the main offices, Hale Prince spoke with Snow White concerning her disapproval of Cinderella's methods. Hale tried to reason with Snow about Cinderella's benefits to the city. Snow would not hear them. She stated Cinderella is a vigilante and must be removed from London in order to provide a safe and secure city for the people. Hale told

Snow he can find a way to get her to meet Cinderella and understand why she is good for the city. Snow disagreed once more and left the office. As she exited the building the Stepsisters, Angelica and Alexis entered the office, seeking to meet with Hale once more.

Cinderella sat still, watching the armed men search for her throughout the warehouse. They finished their third attempt at searching and she was nowhere in their sights. One of the armed men entered the room, telling the others Anne asked for them to stand down, as the Huntsman she called is on his way. Cinderella was confused. A Huntsman? Looking for her, she asked herself. She sighed and jumped down on the floor in front of the men, attacking them from all open corners. Taking them out as she had done before, she fled from the warehouse, running outside and when she stopped, she saw a figure staring at her, wielding an axe.

"Who are you supposed to be?" She asked.

"You must be this Cinderella I've been informed about." The figure said, walking into the lights of the streets.

"Ah." Cinderella replied. "You're the Huntsman I heard about."

"I've been brought here to eliminate you. It is my duty."

Cinderella stepped into a pose. Moving her coat back from her legs. Her fists out and her feet placed. The Huntsman scoffed, holding out the axe.

"You get the first hit." Cinderella said.

III

<u>DO YOU BELIEVE IN FAIRY TALES?</u>

Cinderella dodged the incoming attack by the Huntsman's axe, which slammed into the concrete of the road. Cindy ran behind him, jumping on his back and pummeling him in the kidneys and ribs. The Huntsman, grunting in pain, grabbed her by her leg and tossed her off.

"You're skilled." The Huntsman said. "Who taught you?"

"A good friend."

Cinderella kicked the Huntsman in the face, he stumbled as she grabbed for his axe. He pulled it away and tackled Cinderella into a nearby wall with his shoulder and swung the axe, colliding into the wall as Cindy ducked out of its path. The Huntsman pulled the axe, discovering it was stuck in between the wall. Cinderella noticed and tossed small daggers into the Huntsman's legs. He yelled, dropping down to his knees.

"Now, just hear me out."

"Why should I?" The Huntsman asked. "I know all there is to know."

"And what is that?"

"You're a criminal in this city. The people want you gone. The authorities are searching for you. That is why I was brought here. To find you and I have. The only thing left is to eliminate you or take you in."

"Well, I'm not being taken to the authorities. They don't know what's truly happening in this city."

"And you do?"

"Yes. The woman who hired you, my stepmother. She is the cause of the crimes in this city. Her men tried to kill me before. Didn't go as planned."

"Nonsense. She appeared to me as a kind woman. Only seeking to get you the help you need."

"No. she's the one who planned all of this. The only way this all stops is if she's eliminated. Her and my stepsisters. They are the cause."

Cinderella looked over to her left, hearing police sirens. The Huntsman sighed, holding onto his axe in the wall. He shook his head.

"If what you're saying is true, I will discover it for myself."

"How? You have two daggers in your legs. You can't walk."

"You are mistaken."

The Huntsman pulled the daggers from his legs and the wounds healed immediately. Cinderella startled as the Huntsman pulled his axe from the wall and stood up facing her.

"I have my ways as well."

The Huntsman looked at the daggers. Smelling the metal. He nodded.

"I will hold on to these. I'm intrigued as to what they're made of."

The sirens increased in volume, getting the Huntsman's attention. He looked over and Cinderella was gone. He scoffed, placing the daggers in his pocket as he walked away from the area just as the police cars drove by.

In a nearby area, Snow White followed the police to the warehouse. While making her way there on the sidewalk, Cinderella appeared before her from the shadows. White paused, aiming a taser toward her.

"You!" She yelled.

"I don't know you." Cinderella said.

"You're her. The Sly Detective they call you."

"Put down the taser."

"No. I've come to London to find you. Here you are. Now, I can take you in. justice will be served."

"Not today."

Cinderella kicked the taser from Snow's hand and punched her. Snow fell to the ground, holding her nose as she gazed the surroundings. Seeing Cinderella had disappeared.

IV

ONE TO REMEMBER

Anne arrived at the warehouse just as the police were going in and out speaking with the armed men. She passed them by as she saw the Huntsman standing guard with several of the men.

"What happened here?" She asked.

"Cinderella was here." The Huntsman replied.

"And where is she now? Did she escape?"

"She walked away.'

"Walked away! How could she have walked away?! You were supposed to take care of her!"

"I did what I could. But, you're wrong about her."

"Oh am I?"

"After our scuffle, we spoke. She told me all I needed to know."

"Did she? She told you about her criminal activities."

"No. I could sense it within her. Her true motives. They aren't set to cause chaos in this city. No. She wants to make London better than it was before she decided to put on the hat and coat. Cinderella is a true hero to this place. I understand she's your stepdaughter and you wish her dead."

"More than anything."

"And that is why I cannot help you. You're consumed with envy, covetousness, greed, and anger. Such impulses I cannot aid in my works."

The Huntsman turned and walked away, hearing Anne screaming words toward him concerning his work and Cinderella. The following day, Snow White had told Hale about her encounter with Cinderella, seeing the bruise on her face. Hale could not reason with Snow any longer. She desired to find Cinderella and to bring her in. The Huntsman had left London, after he was paid by Hale in the full price Anne had set for him. For Anne, she had traveled far from London to a small island near the Netherlands. There, she had a meeting with a woman, cloaked in all black, wearing a crystalline-gold crown. The meeting was simple, Anne wanted Cindy dead and the woman agreed to take the mission upon her own hands.

"You will do as the Huntsman should've done?" Anne asked. "Are you sure of it?"

"I'm a woman of my word. I take my missions seriously and I complete them at any cost."

Anne nodded with a dark grin.

"This is better. Much better."

"A Queen does as she desires."

HEAVEN HAS CALLED:
THE BOOKS OF THE HORRORS

I

BEWARE MANY BOOKS

Travis Vail, the Spirit-Seeker cracked open the door to an abandoned home during a late evening. A quiet one. The home was far from the standard suburbs of a city or town. Vail entered the home, seeing nothing but damaged furniture and torn walls. The floors creaked with every footstep he took. He walked through the rooms, going down the hallway toward what appeared to be the office area.

"There it is."

Vail entered the office and went straightforward to the portrait on the wall. The portrait was of a large field with two figures standing in the midst of follies. Vail pulled the portrait off the wall, finding a safe. Vail used his wits to find the code, unlocking the safe. Once he opened it, he saw the safe was empty.

"The hell?"

Vail searched through the office, not finding what he was truly searching for. He sighed.

"They're gone." Vail uttered to himself. "The books are gone."

Vail exited the home, while on the phone speaking with Dr. Galen Donovan concerning the books. Donovan told Vail the books should've been in the house for centuries after being left there by a powerful psychic. Vail suggested the books might've been taken and sold. However, Donovan had an alternative.

"Have you felt the strangeness in the air recently?"

"I have?" Vail replied. "You believe the books are responsible?"

"If they are, it would only imply they were stolen and are being used by some powerful forces."

"You think Balthazar may have them?"

"Not likely. To use the books properly, it would take more than one man to get them operating. It would need a team of many."

"I'll pay Abraham a visit. See what he knows. He has some of the books in his center."

Vail entered his car and drove from the premises. As he went further down the road, a silhouette of a figure stood at the window of the home. Watching the Spirit-Seeker drive away.

II

THE HORROR, THE HORROR

Gabriel Abraham walked through the Revelation Center while Andrea Coralline and Evan Wyatt sat at the desk, researching files pertaining to vampires. The front doors bolted open, snatching their attention and focus. Abraham turned around to see Vail entering the Center. Vail waved with a nod.

"I know you weren't expecting me, lads. But, this is of most importance."

"What's happened now?" Abraham asked.

"Some grimoires have been taken from a secret stash. That stash being an abandoned home that belonged to a long-time past psychic."

"Grimoires?" Evan said. "Are you sure they were such books?"

"I would know for certain. Anyway, we need to find these books and fast."

"Well, it's strange you've come and spoke of a similar action."

"What are you speaking of, Gabriel?"

"Grimoires here have been taken as well. After we dealt with the Vampire Lord, it appeared someone or something infiltrated the Center and took the books. Currently, we're not sure where they are or who has them."

Vail nodded.

"You know this isn't a coincidence. Someone has stolen the books from certain locations. Gathering them together. With those books together, they could cause a dire stray across the world. Everything could very well end as we know it."

"Maybe it was just a thief looking to get rich." Andrea noted. "I mean, that's what one of them would do."

"By any chance have you checked the library here in D.C.?" Vail asked Gabriel.

"No. perhaps, we can head there and see what we find."

"Noted. Then let's get going."

Vail and Abraham headed out to the library in downtown D.C. Once inside, they made way toward the New Age section of the library, Vail realized the people would place grimoires in such a spot. They found the section and began searching. Skimming through the books on the shelves from top to bottom, they found nothing. Vail sighed.

"This is not good."

"I know."

They stood talking about alternatives and behind approached a man. Well-dressed in suit and slacks. He was middle-aged and clean-shaven. Vail could smell the scent of cologne on him. Abraham was unsure who the man was, yet he was keenly aware of their reasons for being in the aisle.

"I see you are searching for something and yet have not found it."

"It happens at time." Vail said. "Good day to you."

"I wouldn't leave just yet Travis Vail." The man said.

Vail turned around slowly.

"How do you know my name?"

"We know you very well. As do you, Gabriel Abraham. My. My. I never thought the day would come where I would meet the infamous Spirit-Seeker and the renown Devilhunter at the same time. Let alone in a public place."

"Who are you?" Abraham asked.

"My name is not important. But who I am associated with is."

"What group are you with? The Cult? The Doctors? One of Demonticronto's followers?"

"I am with the *Mythologists*."

"The Mythologists?" Abraham replied. "Never heard of them."

"I have." Vail said. "Only heard of their name. never seen them or encountered them. But, today has ruled that out. This man claims to be with the Mythologists. So, why are you here?"

"I am here to tell the two of you there's no need in searching for the books. They're in good hands."

Vail stepped forward toward the Mythologist. Abraham prepared himself for the possible altercation. The Mythologist himself was very calm. No fear in his eyes.

"Where are the books?" Vail questioned.

"My master has them."

"Your master?"

"He has plans to use them to shape a better world."

"One man cannot harness the power of those books."

"He knows. That's why he has brought in an associate."

"Associate?" Abraham said. "Who else could manage that kind of power?"

"A greater kind. But, you'll know eventually."

The Mythologist walked away, he turned back toward them with a grin on his face.

"Best to prepare yourselves for what's ahead. The world is about to have a drastic turn of events."

The Mythologist had walked away, leaving Vail and Abraham mediating on plans and theories. Vail clapped his hands, getting the attention of the others in the library by accident. He waved them off.

"What's next?" Abraham said.

"We gather everyone." Vail replied. "We gather the team."

III

A GREATER KIND

Without haste, Vail and Abraham sent out word to gather the team together. With the aid of the Visitant Outlander and Dark Manhunter, they were able to teleport several of the members to the Revelation Center for the meeting. Vail and Abraham waited for the team to arrive and two bright flashes of light emitted within the lobby of the Center and out of the first flash came Outlander with Cinderella and the Ghost of England. The second flash walked out Manhunter with Creed, Death Chaser, and Papa Afterlife. Vail looked around as the light dimmed out.

"Where's the other lad?"

"Who?" Cinderella asked.

"The one with the white mark on his chest?"

"He has other matters to attend to." Afterlife said. "You have heard about the 'Steeler Incident' haven't you?"

"Not to my knowledge. No."

"Terror will be fine. We're enough for this task."

"Depends on who we're facing." Abraham noted. "Anyone have any clues?"

"Signs of the books have been felt throughout the universe. Both naturally and spiritually." Outlander stated. "Those who have them are gaining knowledge and power from them. Shaking the fabric of reality in total."

"I did hear about a stash somewhere in Manchester. "Cinderella said. "It was taken from some place."

"Then, you can lead us there." Vail said.

"I don't operate in Manchester, Trav. That's the other guy."

"What other guy?" Abraham asked.

"She's talking about the Fable bloke."

"Never heard of him."

"Few have." Cinderella replied. "Anyhow, that's where one stash was located."

"Ok. Anyone know of any other places?"

"Well, we only know two." Vail said. "Manchester and somewhere here in D.C."

"True."

"There is another place surging with energy." Manhunter spoke. "It's in a deep cemetery. Guarded by a restless spirit."

"Where is this cemetery?" Creed asked.

"Deep in Ireland."

"I see." Vail said. "Looks like we'll all be doing some traveling."

"How are we going to get to these places as quickly as possible?" Abraham wondered. "How will it be done. Not all of us can teleport."

Vail clapped his hands together with a smirk.

"I have the idea. We split up into teams. I'll led one over to the UK, find out about the books in Manchester while you, Gabriel, take a team and head on out to find out more about these Mythologists."

"It'll work. But, it still doesn't conclude the travel."

"I will aid Vail." Manhunter said.

"Then, I shall accompany Abraham's unit."

Vail nodded. "Then, it's settled."

"Now, who's going with who?" Abraham asked.

"Shaw and I will go with Vail." Cinderella said.

"I will accompany you as well." Death Chaser added.

"Fair point." Vail nodded.

"Creed and I will join Abraham and Outlander." Afterlife said.

"Everyone knows what they must do?" Vail said. "Good."

"I met a young man in London who had an encounter with the Mythologists." Outlander said.

"So, myself, Cindy, and Shaw will speak with him once we leave Manchester."

"I cannot allow that. the young man must see me. That way he will not be in fear."

Vail nodded.

"I understand."

Vail went and walked toward the door, stopping as everyone began heading out. Cinderella approached him, seeing something was on his mind.

"Those words." Vail uttered. "How could I have let them slip."

"What is it?"

"Me and Abraham met a fellow from the Mythologists. He told us they were working with someone outside of their group."

"Any chance you may know who it is?"

"I do now. The Mythologist said their helper was of a greater kind."

"A greater kind? I'm not getting what that means."

"It means Vernon Lance is working with them and that is trouble for all of us."

"The Satanist?"

"Yes. We need to find the books now."

IV

THE CON MAGE OF MANCHESTER

A portal opened in an alleyway in the city of Manchester with Vail, Cinderella, Shaw, Chaser, and Manhunter walking out. As the portal closed, they each looked at the location in which they stood.

"Recognize this spot?" Vail asked Cinderella.

"No. Should I?"

"Might as well see what's on the end of this alleyway." Vail replied.

They followed him through the alley, reaching the outer parts, seeing a bar just up ahead. Vail looked around, seeing the vehicles driving on the street, yet on one side of the road, construction was being done. Vail pointed toward it.

"What happened there?"

"Maybe a wreck." Cinderella replied.

"A wreck would not have caused that much damage." Shaw added. Something happened here and not long ago."

Death Chaser turned his focus toward the bar behind them. Sensing an energy coming from within. He pointed as Manhunter also was sensing the energy.

"The bar." Chaser said. "Something's inside."

Vail and Cinderella walked forward, facing the bar. Hey keened their senses. Cinderella knew there was something strange with the bar, while Vail shrugged his shoulders and walked.

"Let's go have ourselves a look-see."

Vail went ahead and entered the bar. Once inside, he saw the bar was filled with magical creatures. Vail spotted an orc near the back of the bar while there was a satyr sitting at the bar drinking whiskey. Cinderella looked around and was amazed. The Chaser entered with Manhunter following and the entire bar went from lively to dead silent. Vail raised his hands.

"Hello lads. Now, we're not from these parts. However, we have come for a purpose. Do any of you know of the Man Called Fable, the bloke who operates in this town?"

Everyone in the bar turned and gave each other looks. Quiet looks. But knowledgeable. The bartender stepped forward as Vail turned toward him.

"Yeah. We know of him."

"Mind you tell us where he might be? We need to speak with him."

The bartender pointed to the further section of the bar near the back. They looked and saw Fable himself sitting at a table, having a drink. Fable looked up toward them, grinned and held up his drink. Vail shook his head, thanking the bartender before approaching Fable's table. Vail and Cinderella stood in front facing Fable. Fable extended his hand at the chairs.

"You guys can sit."

Vail and Cinderella sat at the table while Shaw, Chaser, and Manhunter stood guard as there were several trolls who were glaring toward Fable.

"Listen, we've never met before." Vail said. "But something has happened which brings us to this moment."

"First off, my guy. Who are you people supposed to be?"

"I'm Travis Vail, Spirit-Seeker. She is Cinderella. While the others are-"

"Cinderella? Bullshit." Fable grinned. "She's not Cinderella. Can't be. Fairy tales don't exist."

"And yet you interact with a realm where such creatures are relative in fairy tales." Cinderella smiled.

"So, you're the one they've been searching for in London."

"I am and I would like it to remain quiet. Until this is all over."

"And what is all this?"

"Some powerful grimoires have been taken. Gathered to cause some major damage to the world. All of creation could suffer if those who have them succeed."

Fable took a drink and shook his head.

"She said something was gone."

"Who said what?" Cinderella asked.

"Oh. Pandora. She told me some books had been taken. I couldn't' find out where but she panicked over it slightly."

"So, what has this Pandora woman found out?"

"Nothing so far. But, the fact the two of you came here asking about grimoires leads me to believe this isn't just a Manchester-only situation."

"It's not."

"Fable, may I ask if you knew where the books were kept?"

"I have no clue. Never saw the books. Only heard of them being stored up in a place by Pandora and those Four fellas."

"What four fellows?" Vail asked.

"Doesn't matter. Look here, I will do what I can to help you guys out with this. By doing this, I'll be helping Pandora and she can stay off my back when it comes to matters like this. I can't take the stress."

Manhunter's cloak began flowing, getting the attention of everyone in the bar. Vail looked up toward him with concerned face.

"What is it?"

"Someone's coming." Manhunter said. "Someone powerful."

A flash of light emitted from the middle of the bar, startling the creatures inside and as the light faded, Vernon Lance stood in its place. Vail jumped from the table, ready for a fight. Cinderella followed and Fable stood up, his hand on the revolver. The Chaser's hands emitted with sinfire, and Shaw was prepared as his body was slowly glowing.

"Who's this guy?" Fable asked.

"Vernon Lance." Vail said. "A thorn in the sides of many."

"It is good to see you again once more, Spirit-Seeker."

"Why are you here?"

"To tell you and your friends something you should know."

"And what is that?"

"The grimoires you are searching for? They belong to me now. Their power already flows within me and soon all of the world will bow before me."

"Is he always like this?" Fable asked.

"Every day." Vail replied.

"What are we going to do?" Cinderella asked.

"You will do nothing." Lance told Cinderella. "Stay away from my work or suffer."

"Suffer what?" Chaser said.

"A greater fate worse than death."

"Meh." Fable said, raising up the revolver and firing a shot.

The round went straight through Lance's body, hitting the shelf at the bar. Vail knew it then. Fable stood confused. Cinderella stepped forward.

"He's not really here." Vail said.

"I know how to operate, Spirit-Seeker. You should've known by now."

Lance faded away from their sight. Vail grunted, pacing in anger.

"We have to find out where he is," Cinderella said. "It's the only way."

"And how are we going to track him down?" Vail asked. "His magic is too powerful now. I can't track him myself. Manhunter, Chaser. Can either of you track him?"

"He's shielded." Manhunter said. "Even from my own eyes and might."

"I cannot trace him." Chaser replied. "Something dark is over him. Hindering my power."

Vail walked toward the door as the others spoke of possible solutions. Fable was well involved. Fable told Cinderella he was no sorcerer and Vail clapped his hands together, returning to the team.

"That's it."

"What is?" Cinderella asked.

"A sorcerer."

"What about one?" Fable asked. "I'm not one."

"Not talking about you. I know one. He may help us."

"When did you meet a sorcerer?" Cinderella questioned.

"Very recently. He helped me with a favor to a family."

Cinderella nodded. "Then, where is this sorcerer?"

"We'll have to check the last place I met him."

"Then let's get going." Fable said. "I'm tagging along for this."

Elsewhere, Abraham's team walked through London during the night, standing outside of the library. Abraham looked around, seeing only civilians walking and going about their night.

"Where is he?" Abraham asked.

"Give me a moment." Outlander replied, extending his arms.

The ground became covered in mists. The civilians had vanished and the vehicles which were passing through were gone. Abraham looked around as did Afterlife and they were astonished by Outlander's feat of power. Creed stood quiet, looking past the mist and he saw someone approaching.

"There." Creed said.

Abraham looked out and saw someone coming toward them. Outlander stepped forward as he saw Jacob Wilson coming through the mist.

"You heard my call." Outlander said.

"I did. Why did you contact me?"

"Because my allies here need to know more about the Mythologists. They have taken something which does not belong to them. In turn, they could very well destroy all of creation if they are not stopped."

Jacob looked behind Outlander, seeing Abraham, Afterlife, and Creed.

"Who are they?"

"Those who you can trust."

"Jacob," Abraham said walking forward. "We just need to know what you know about them. Like the kind of places they meet up. Where do they operate out of? You know anything of them?"

"Primarily, they meet at all kinds of places. Restaurants, city halls, schools, stores. But, they mostly operate out of museums or libraries. That's where they keep their collections."

"Museums. Libraries. Ah, I should've known." Abraham replied. 'They've been sitting under our noses the whole time."

"At least you have your answer." Outlander said. "You did well, Jacob Wilson."

"We need to return to D.C." Abraham said.

"We cannot." Afterlife replied. "We have to reach the cemetery first. Find the books hidden there."

Abraham nodded. "You are correct. Let's get going. See you around, Mr. Wilson."

Jacob nodded as Outlander opened the portal for them to exit the area. As the portal closed, the surroundings returned to normal. Jacob looked around, seeing familiar events as before. He chuckled under his breath before walking away.

V

A SUPREME ENCHANTER
AND
A RESTORATION MAN

Vail led his team to the source of his information, following a path of peculiar magic within the air. Unseen by the natural eyes. With Manhunter and Chaser's assistance, Vail led them toward the Citadel of enchantment. Fable looked on at the structure.

"Where did this place come from?"

"It's been here." Vail said. "For a very long time."

"Do we knock or wait?" Cinderella asked.

"He'll know we're here." Vail replied.

"Who's he?" Fable wondered.

The doors of the Citadel opened and out of them came down Doctor Fortune, levitating down the stairs toward them as his cloak flowed with the wind. He saw Vail and nodded with a smile. Vail nodded back as Fortune measured the others. He looked at Chaser with a keen eye.

"A Soul of Retribution. Nice to meet one of you."

"You know of us?"

"I know of all of you. Robert Shaw, I am familiar with the events that made you what you are this day. Make no mistake, you will have your vengeance soon."

"I am honored of your words."

"I've heard of the stories across London of a sneaky individual. Famed by the fairy tales that proclaim your existence. Now, I stand before you, Cinderella."

"I'm not as detailed as the stories suggest." Cinderella grinned.

"I can very well see that." Fortune replied. "Manhunter, I know of your purpose and I know of your hatred to those of magic."

"Then, you know what I aspire to do."

"I do. However, we are not here to fight one another. Regardless of our paths. It seems Travis Vail has brought you all here for a reason. Vail, I would like the know that reason."

"I must guess you've felt a strangeness in the air. Reeking of some dark power?"

"I have. Me and my apprentice have been studying its paths. It's bouncing across the sky like I've never seen before."

"Because it's energy from powerful grimoires."

"What do these grimoires suggest?"

"Vernon Lance, a powerful priest in the Satanic field has them in his possession with the group calling themselves the Mythologists. I don't know what they're after, but I know why Lance is involved. He's seeking to become powerful. Much more powerful."

"What is your plan currently?" Fortune wondered.

"We don't have one exactly. The others are already heading to the cemetery to find the third stash of grimoires."

"So, Lance and the Mythologists have the first two stashes in their hands?"

"Correct." Vail said. "We need to know how to weaken the power that comes from them. By doing so, we'll weaken Lance and the Mythologists will cower in fear of what's to come."

"Books such as those should not be in the same place at the same time. Explains the darkness above the earth. The solution is simple. Separate them from each other."

"Wait." Cinderella said. "That's all? Just separate them?"

"Yes. How many grimoires are there?"

"Five from each stash." Vail replied. "Lance and company currently have ten."

"While the remaining five are in some cemetery." Fortune nodded. "Understood. I will help you find Lance and these Mythologists. You face them and scatter the books across the four corners of the earth. You do that, the task is done."

"Lance is too powerful for us to face head-on." Vail said. "we need some assistance."

"You're asking for my help in this endeavor?"

"You helped me with Carrie. I'm just asking, help with this. If Lance succeeds, all of creation could very well end. I know you cannot allow something as powerful as that to happen."

Fortune nodded, turning back toward the citadel.

"When the time comes, you will have me on your side." Fortune replied. "Right now, do what you must do."

Fortune entered the Citadel as the doors closed behind him. Fable threw his arms up, looking around the forest area behind them.

"So, that's it?" Fable asked. "He's not going to help out?"

"Fortune's a trustworthy guy." Vail said. "He'll help out. He already said it."

"We need to return to the others." Manhunter said. "Gather ourselves together and confront Vernon Lance and the Mythologists."

"Then let's return to D.C." Vail said.

Over in Ireland, Abraham's team arrived at the cemetery. A foggy and damp night. The cemetery had a presence of its own. A crawling sense tingled down their backs aside from Outlander and Creed. Abraham searched for the sight, but was unable to track it down. Outlander extended his right hand across the cemetery and one peculiar grave with an unnamed headstone shined like the sun.

"There it is." Outlander said.

They reached the grave, seeing it had appeared to have been dug up recently. Abraham sighed.

"No sign of the books."

"No." Creed said. "The books are here."

"How do you know?" Afterlife wondered.

"Because he has them." Creed pointed in front of them.

They looked out and a decomposed hand arose from the ground. The trembling feeling underneath them shook the cemetery and from the hand arose a head and a body. The figure stood above the ground, standing at the same height as Abraham and Afterlife. Dressed in rags of clothing, ripped pants, torn shoes. Its hair long and white. White as snow. Its eyes soulless, yet there is some form of life within them. Piercing through the veil. Creed's cloak spread widely, flowing with caution, Afterlife's hands became covered in smoke while Abraham steadied himself. Outlander stepped forward toward the figure.

"I know what they call you." Outlander said. "The Restoration Man."

"I cannot be killed." The Restoration Man said.

"True. we are not here to fight you. We seek the books. Where are they?"

"Why should I give them to you?"

"Because you do want to know what the second death feels like." Outlander replied. "Not yet anyway."

The Restoration Man paused himself. Stepping back behind the unnamed headstone. Creed noticed and rushed over, knocking the stone over to reveal the books.

"There." Creed said.

Abraham went over and grabbed the books. He nodded to the others. The Restoration Man stepped back as Outlander kept his eyes on him.

"You do well with those." Restoration Man said.

"We know what must be done." Outlander said. "Return to your service, fleshly spirit."

Outlander opened the portal and they returned to the Revelation Center where Vail and the others waited.

VI

A PRIEST IN THE BOOK

Vail stood inside the Center with the others just as Abraham returned with the books. Vail smirked.

"You found them."

"Yeah. What did you guys come up with and who's that?"

"I'm known as Fable. Some call me The Man Called Fable."

"Why is a stranger in this place?"

"He's here to help. Seriously. He's been tracking down the books himself."

"We have all that we need." Chaser said. "Now, let's find Vernon Lance and end this."

"That's a good idea." Vail said. "Only where do we find them?"

"At the library." Abraham said. "That's where they are."

"How are you certain of that?" Shaw questioned.

"Because it's what the young Wilson had given us." Outlander said. "He's familiar with their movements. He would know where they operate."

"And you rust the young one?" Manhunter asked. "So blindly?"

"It is not blindness, Manhunter. It is justice."

"Only when you're betrayed for a just cause."

"Now, there's no need to stir each other up." Vail said. "Save it for the fight ahead."

"We need to get the library now." Creed spoke. "End all of this."

"I agree with the darkly gruesome one." Fable said. "Let's find these guys, finish all of this so we can all return to our lives."

"He's right." Cinderella said. "I'm sure someone in London needs my help right now.:

"Eh, alright." Vail mumbled. "Let's get going. Teleporting again?"

"No other choice." Manhunter said.

The group teleported themselves into the library late in the night.

Upon their arrival, they found themselves facing off against strange shadow figures. Vail knew Lance has summoned them to keep the library guarded. Immediately the library became a place of war. Creed, Chaser, and Shaw took the fight to the shadow figures while Vail, Cinderella, Abraham, Afterlife, Fable went ahead as Outlander and Manhunter used their power to shroud the library from the public eyes. For when a civilian passed by the library, they only saw the emptiness within. The lights appeared off and the library seemed closed to their natural eyes.

"Where could they be?" Vail questioned.

"Downstairs." Abraham said. "I'm sure of it."

They went forward, finding themselves in what appeared to be an exceptionally large room. Large enough to be kept hidden from the public. Within the room were the Mythologists who were sitting in a circle, their heads were down with Lance standing before them.

"Your games end here, Lance." Vail yelled. "Give us the books."

"And why should I do such a thing when the plan is fully coming into motion?"

"Enough of your words." Fable said. "We're here for the books. Hand them over."

"Or what?" Lance grinned.

"You know what to do." Vail told the team.

They all rushed toward Lance without haste. Lance turned toward them as the Mythologists themselves did not move as Lance raised his hand toward them, stopping them in their tracks. He laughed as eh tossed them back to where they entered. Lance scoffed, returning to the books as they were opened.

"I'm not stopping here." Vail said, raising himself up.

"Keep coming, Spirit-Seeker. I will always knock you down. It is our fate."

"It is. But, it could use an extra hand." Vail said, stepping back.

Within the room streaked a bolt of lightning and from the lightning appeared Pandora alongside Doctor Fortune. Fable looked on, seeing Pandora. She turned toward him and nodded. Fable nodded back in respect as Fortune stared down Lance, seeing the Mythologists on the ground and the books ahead.

"This has come to an end, Priest." Fortune said.

"A Supreme Enchanter." Lance scoffed. "More power must I receive this night."

"Not likely."

Pandora whipped her hands around forming a magical bind, causing the Mythologists to rise from the ground and attack Lance. While she held her power upon them, Fortune quickly pulled the books toward him as Lance let out a loud yell. Vail saw what was happening and ran toward Lance, but Cinderella grabbed his arm.

"What are you doing, Cindy?"

"Now is not the time for your anger to get the better of you. Fortune has the books. We can go now."

"No. I cannot let Lance escape. Not this time."

Vail went to move ahead, and Cinderella kept her hold on him. Fortune appeared to him with the books in hand.

"We must go, Travis Vail. Pandora can only hold them for so long."

Vail looked out, string at Lance. Vernon saw him and smirked while fighting off the Mythologists. Vail sighed as they left the room through Fortune's wormhole. The Mythologists ceased their attack and fell to the floor. Lance looked around, seeing the books were gone as were his adversaries. He screamed as the floor beneath him opened and he went down into the darkness, only with his laughter to echo out into the open.

Afterwards, they gathered at the Center where Fortune spoke to Vail and Abraham, telling them the books must be scattered by only five of them across the earth. To keep them hidden from humanity and other forces which seek to do harm. Vail took three, Abraham took three, Fable took three, Outlander took three, and Manhunter took the remaining three. They all went and scattered the books to various locations which will not be named. Only the ones who scattered the books will know the locations of the earth.

Returning to their own lives and operations a day later, Vail kept his ears and eyes open for Lance's return. Fable and Pandora returned to the Rift to meet with Chernabog concerning Emblem, Abraham went ahead with his studies with Andrea and Evan, Afterlife returned to educate the Yonderers, Creed kept his spiritual senses keened for Adrambadon's return as did Chaser with Demonticronto. Cinderella returned to London, finding a search warrant out for her arrest, Shaw had wandered throughout London and the spiritual plane alongside Outlander and Manhunter. The two figures hovered above the earth, looking down.

"Do you believe they'll manage to take on what's to come?" Outlander asked.

"In time, we will see what makes of them." Manhunter replied. "For I know we both are certain they will be ready when the war begins."

"As will we."

DOCTOR DARK: DARKNESS AND LIGHT

I

THE FOOTSTEPS OF ONE MANY FEARS

Standing in the realm of the Astral Dimension, Darkous looks upon Michael The Archangel. The two discuss with one another about the previous victory over Mazakala and how much they have to repair in order to avoid another event with his release in the near future.

"There is another command that has presented itself to you, Darkous." Michael said.

"What has been commanded of me?"

"After the events of your battle with Mazakala, there have been incidents occurring throughout the realms of the darkness and the light. We know that only you should be given this task to discover what is truly happening across the cosmos."

Darkous nodded.

"I will begin on this task as soon as possible."

Michael nodded and flew up in the air, exiting the Astral Dimensional realm of existence. Darkous prepared himself mentally for the task at his hand and exited the Astral Dimension, heading first to Earth.

On Earth, Carol Hunters, the supernatural reporter continues her studies of the occult, diving into more knowledge that she was aware of in her early beginnings of research. She later came upon a series of old documents from the museum that contained information that she recognized from the men within the museum who call themselves the

Mythologists.

"I am curious as to what they are talking about." Carol said.

Carol continued studying and was tempted to contact Malach HaMavet for more details concerning the Mythologists, but decided on waiting to find more information before telling Malach about the circumstances in order to have herself prepared for what could possibly happen.

Darkous moved across the earth. Day and night. Going from country to country. He searches the ancient lands of old, finding nothing that would be tampering with the darkness and light powers. While going through the lands during nightfall, Darkous could feel a uncertain energy coming from the homes of people. Darkous stopped by at one person's home and entered in through the door, walking through it like a living vapor of mist.

"The energy here." Darkous said. "It is of another realm."

Darkous walked upstairs in the home, seeing the bedrooms of two children, a girl and a boy. Down the hall was the bedroom of their parents. Darkous could feel the energy surrounding them all, but the energy was strong on the little girl. He entered her room and walked toward her, seeing her fully asleep.

"What is happening amongst you, young one."

Darkous placed his right hand onto the little girl's head and instantly, he entered her dream. Within her dream was the little girl playing with friends in a yard. Her brother was seen walking amongst them. Darkous looked around, feeling the energy growing in strength.

He looked toward a tree and spotted a being staring at the young girl with piercing eyes.

"What are you?" Darkous said walking toward the being.

The entity glared at Darkous and vanished into the air with a swift blow of wind. Darkous looked around, not able to find the being and turned back to the young girl, still playing amongst her friends and brother. Darkous exited her dream and entered her brother's dream. The dream of the brother was different, involving a room covered in video games and action figures. The boy played with the figures along with the being from the girl's dream. Darkous approached the being.

"Tell me what you are."

The being turned to Darkous and smiled before vanishing. Darkous turned to the little boy and he stared at him.

"Where did my friend go?" The little boy asked.

"I don't think he was your friend, young one."

Darkous left the boy's dream and proceed to enter the parents' dream. Within their dream was a crowded interstate. They were in their car with their son and daughter in the back. Darkous walked through the street of the crowed roadway.

"So many stopped." Darkous said. "So many trapped."

Darkous could see the being once again standing in front of the road, causing the traffic jam. Darkous hovered up and flew toward the being. In great speed, Darkous tacked the being and rushed him into one of the cars.

"Tell me what you are now!" Darkous said.

"I'm what the little ones fear." The entity said. "I'm what their parents teach them of the night. I am what keeps them in line during the night."

"Your name." Darkous said. "Tell me your name, entity?"

"I'm the Bogeyman." He said with a smile on his face. Showing his decaying teeth.

Darkous released the Bogeyman as he vanished once again. Darkous exited the dream of the parents and left the home. After several hours going through the earth, Darkous discovered the Bogeyman had been traveling through the dreams of many. Tormenting them to the point of even killing in his running spree.

Darkous returned to the Astral Dimension and Beatrice is waiting on him. She sees the purpose in his eyes and can feel that something is taking place throughout the realms of the cosmos.

"I can sense some power going through the cosmos, Darkous."

"It's a power of torment and fear." Darkous said. "The Bogeyman is freely roaming the earth."

"The Bogeyman?" Beatrice said. "I thought he was killed during the early purge."

"Apparently not. He survived the purge and has made himself known once again. Now, I have to deal with him and the events taking place within the darkness and light."

"What do you have in mind concerning The Bogeyman?"

"I have to visit an old associate of ours."

"Who would that be exactly?"

"I'm going to the Patchlands."

Beatrice looked at Darkous as if he said something that made her feel ignorant of her place.

"You're not considering working with him again are you?" Beatrice said. "You know how cunning he can be toward us and those above."

"True. But, he knows the Bogeyman more than most would assume him to know. He could be of useful assistance."

Darkous prepared himself to head out for the Patchlands.

"Make sure you keep your awareness keen."

"I will. Surely."

Darkous hovered into the air, leaving the Astral Dimension as if he was a gust of wind during a thunderstorm.

II

PUMPKIN LANGUAGE

Entering the Patchlands during the brink of day, Darkous comes down from the sky, seen from the ground like a horde of bats or crows. Walking through the trails of the Patchlands was a figure that resembled a man but possessed a pumpkin for a head. Darkous stood on the ground walking towards the man.

"Mr. Pumpkinhead." Darkous said.

He turned and faced Darkous. His face showing a smile as he laid down his rake and approached the Keeper of the Cosmos.

"The Shrouded One makes himself known unto me in my own realm."

"I do and I come with a purpose of intent."

"Such as?"

"How much do you know of The Bogeyman?"

"I know much about him. His power, his hobbies, his lusts. I know much about him to tell dozens of stories with."

"I need to know all that you know."

"Why would you want to know all about The Bogeyman?"

"Because he's out there causing torment amongst the sleeping ones during the nightfall."

Mr. Pumpkinhead nodded.

"Ah. So, he has been released you're saying. I thought he was dead and gone."

"That is what we all assumed. But, we were wrong."

"I will help you, but it will involve you going in several directions to find your answers."

"You're sending me on a puzzle quest?"

"In a matter of yes or no, I am."

"What will be in possession of these quests?"

"The answers you seek concerning The Bogeyman. Don't worry, you might have some fun in this. I know I would."

"Go back to your harvesting, Pumpkinhead. I will find what I need in your trails."

Darkous took his first step toward the first trail in searching for the knowledge of The Bogeyman. Mr. Pumpkinhead watched him walk forward and smirked.

"Wait till he sees what's in store for him. Ha!"

Back on Earth, Carol meets with Malach HaMavet inside of his cabin as she brought along her detailed and studies concerning the Mythologists. Malach looked at her findings, within the books she carried along the way and the papers of notes that she written.

"How long did it take you to study all of this?" Malach said.

"It took some time." Carol said. "I had nothing to do other than put my time into learning who those men are and what they're planning in the shadows."

"How are you feeling, exactly?"

"What do you mean?"

"I mean, how do you feel after seeing that horde in the streets a while back."

"Oh. It laid an effect on me that I probably will never have removed. But, it showed me there's more to this world than what we see with our own eyes."

"Trust me when I say this to you, what you seen is only a small drop in the sea to what is really out there."

Carol smiled as she laid her eyes back onto her findings.

On the Patchlands trail, Darkous walked through, looking around at the fields of plentiful harvest. He could see what appeared to be portals into parts of the earth. Within those portals were images of people sleeping and The Bogeyman circling them around their bed, tormenting them in their sleep.

"He circles them. Why?"

As Darkous walked, a bolt of light flash in front of him. Halting his steps. Darkous walked through the light and swiftly wiped it away with his hand. He looked forward seeing two figures that appeared to be made of light.

"Who are you?" Darkous said.

"We were sent here to halt your findings on The Bogeyman." One figure said. "You cannot learn more about him."

"I will."

Darkous raised his hand and from it was released a small wave of energy that knocked the two figures on their back. They looked at Darkous with fear in their eyes.

"But, you cannot learn more. We promised him we would keep you away."

"Who is him?" Darkous said. "Tell me his name and I will deal with him."

"We will not speak his name." The other figure said. "He might destroy us from existence."

"His name. Now."

"We... we will not speak it."

Darkous stared at the two figures. No emotion on his face as his eyes are locked onto them and his pupils turning a dim blue.

"Very well."

Darkous raised his arms up toward the sky and above the two figures emerged a thick cloud of darkness. The two figures started firing blasts of light bolts toward the cloud. Having no effect except causing the cloud to grow in size, covering more ground.

"Please stop the cloud!"

"I will not." Darkous said. "You two have made your decision."

The cloud came down upon the two figures and swallowed them up. The faint sounds of their screams could be heard before silken came in. Darkous walked past the cloud and continued on forward down the trail.

"This is no matter of games."

Further down the trail way, Darkous finds himself surrounded by a group of shadow creatures. Darkous shook his head and released a small sigh. He looked at the shadow creatures.

"Do you know who you're surrounding?" Darkous said. "From the very realm you were birthed from, I rule."

"It doesn't matter now." One shadow creature said. "You're on our turf now."

"I see what I must do in order to make you understand."

Darkous released several shadow creatures of his own and they combated against the shadow creatures of the trail. Darkous stood by and watched the fighting commencing before him.

"Finish them off." Darkous said to his shadow creatures. "Send them on their way back home."

The shadow creatures of Darkous instantly killed the shadow creatures of the trail and they vanished into the air with a gust of wind. Darkous continued walking down the trail and spoke to himself.

"Something is not right. What has Pumpkinhead sent me on?"

After finishing the trail, Darkous returned to the Astral Dimension to take further looks across the cosmos in search of The Bogeyman. From behind him walked Beatrice. She looked at him as if he made some mistake. He glanced at her.

"I know what I did, Beatrice."

"You were taken for a fool by Pumpkinhead."

"I am aware of that. Though, the portal that showed the humans sleeping was no folly play. It was real and it confirms to me that The Bogeyman is still on earth. He hasn't left the earth because he cannot at this particular time."

"You think Pumpkinhead may know what Bogeyman needs to escape from being earthbound?"

"I think I do. You mind coming along with me?"

"With pleasure."

Mr. Pumpkinhead sat inside of his home on the Patchlands and the front door opened with a gust of wind. Pumpkinhead looked over toward the door and stood up, walking towards it to close it.

"Damn wind."

Pumpkinhead placed his hand on the door and closed it. He turned around and was stopped to see both Darkous and Beatrice standing inside of his home. He pointed at them while laughing.

"So, the wind that blew my door open. That was the both of you?"

"It was." Beatrice said.

"My, my. Don't you Astrals have amazing feats."

"We're not here to discuss feats, Pumpkinhead." Darkous said.

"Why are you both here? You again mostly."

"Don't take me for a fool." Darkous said. "You sent me on some folly trail surrounded with small diversions to keep me ignorant of the knowledge of The Bogeyman."

"Oh. You discovered what I was doing all along, huh. Funny."

"It is not something to laugh at." Beatrice said. "We need to know all there is about Bogeyman."

"Wouldn't it be best if you only left him alone. He's stuck on earth for holy's sake."

Darkous walked toward Pumpkinhead and snatched him by his throat, shoving him against the wall of his home.

"Give us what we came for or suffer a fate that is worse than a blinding light."

"Ok." Pumpkinhead said. "Alright, I'll give you what you want. Just let me back on the ground."

"Sure." Darkous said as he dropped Pumpkinhead onto his feet.

Pumpkinhead was crouched on the ground, catching his breath and gazing up at Darkous and Beatrice.

"Fair play." Pumpkinhead said. "Fair indeed."

"The knowledge!" Darkous said. "Speak it now."

"Sure. The reason why The Bogeyman is out and tormenting the humans is to find a way back to his plane of existence called the Dreamscape."

"The Dreamscape?" Beatrice said. "I thought that place was destroyed during the Purge."

"Apparently, my darling, it was not." Pumpkinhead said. "It was locked down to keep The Bogeyman from entering back into the realm. He derives his power and strength from that place."

"The Bogeyman is only trying to find his way back home?" Darkous said. "That is what you're telling me, Pumpkinhead?"

"That is what I'm telling you, Shrouded One. For right now, he is weak. Too weak to fight against those against him. But, if he finds his way back into the Dreamscape, he will be more powerful than he ever could be."

"We thank you for this information, Pumpkinhead." Darkous said. "We will meet again."

"Anytime, Astrals."

Darkous and Beatrice vanished into the thin air. Pumpkinhead sighed as he sat back down into his chair and continued to smoke his pipe.

III

MYTHOS TO EXPLORE

In her apartment, Carol read a newspaper that contain some information regarding a secret meeting between the men whom she knows as the Mythologists. The city is calling them the Bankers. They are scheduled to have a bank meeting amongst themselves and a few selected others during the day. Carol knows that there is more to the story and contacts Malach to aid her in discovering what is truly taking place at City Hall.

Carol traveled to the City Hall and saw the Mythologists sitting amongst each other. She proceeded to approach them, but one spotted her. Smoking his cigar, he looked at Carol and remembered her from their previous meeting before.

"I remember you, lady." He said.

"You… you do?"

"I do. Come over here and sit with us for a brief moment."

"Ok."

Carol sat down with the Mythologists. Shaken up a bit and hesitant to speak a word that might get her in trouble. She looked at what they were reading and it was an ancient grimoire. She pointed at it and the Mythologist looked and turned toward her.

"Do you know what that is?"

"I do not."

The Mythologist chuckled. He grabbed the grimoire and handed it to her. She grabbed the book and opened it, seeing it covered in spells and invocations. She looked at the Mythologist with uncertain ease.

"Is this a spell book?"

"It is. We found it amongst this old place. Makes you think how the politicians win their elections, huh."

"It does in a way. What do you guys intend on doing with it?"

"Ma'am, what we do with this book is none of your concern. But, I'll give you a little insight into what we have planned with it."

The Mythologist leaned toward her, his breath the smell of ash and smoke, covering the scent of his cologne.

"There's a certain figure that lurks in the dreams of Man. His power is beyond what average humans are aware of. We intend on bringing him here to aid us in our mission. To grant us entrance into his realm."

"Your mission?"

"Creating a new order of the world. Cleaning it up from its foul and awful stench of human selfishness and emotions. We have to do it because we're the only ones who can."

"How can you do it?"

"With this book, we will conjure up our figure. He will tell us of his realm and will aid us in entering the Third Heaven."

"The Third Heaven?"

"Yes. The highest of all the realms. The domain of the Eternal One."

"But, how could you do that? You do understand that you said the Eternal One."

"I did. There are powers that are at work that can do marvelous things for those who use it properly."

"So, that bank meeting that was in the newspaper, that was for show?"

"Of course, we had to come up with a diversion to keep the commoners away from knowing our real intent."

"Maybe they could help in some way."

"No ma'am, they cannot help us. They cannot help you and they certainly cannot help themselves. They are lost and they need order in guidance."

Carol looked at her watch, seeing the time. She stood up from the chair and the Mythologist grabbed her arm. Frightening her, he looked into her eyes.

"I will grant you an invite to our little get tighter this evening. If you desire to learn more."

Carol nodded with a faint smile.

"I would love to."

"Splendid."

"Will I have to ask for your name?"

"My name." The Mythologist said with a laugh. "We have no names. Only purpose."

Carol nodded.

"We will see you tonight, ma'am."

"Yes you will."

Carol left City Hall and contacted Malach on her phone.

"Malach, I have to speak with you and its very important that we do it immediately."

"Come by the cabin and we can discuss it all there." Malach said.

"Sure."

Carol hung up the phone and left in her car, going to Malach's cabin. Carol later made it to Malach's cabin. Malach, already sitting outside, sees her approach. He stood up and opened the front door as she walked toward him.

"How bad is it, Carol?" Malach said.

"I would pick worse over bad."

Both of them walk into the cabin and Malach closes the door. Inside, Carol sits down at his table and Malach sits alongside her.

"Tell me what you came here to speak."

"I met with the Mythologists."

"Again?"

"One spotted me and allowed me to sit with them for a moment. He told me of their meeting tonight."

"What of their meeting?"

"They had a book. It contained spells and invocations. He told me they're going to use it tonight to conjure up some being that inhabits the dreams of people. Said that he would grant them entrance into his realm and would help them enter the Third Heaven."

"Wait, wait, wait." Malach said standing up. "The Third Heaven?"

"That's what he told me."

"This isn't good. Even if they can't breach The Third Heaven, they'll still cause harm to the cosmos. We need more help."

"But, who's this being that inhabits dreams? I'm unaware right now."

"The Bogeyman." Malach said. "They're going to conjure him up."

"The Bogeyman's real?"

"Yes, he is and funny enough, my Master has been searching for him."

"You think he'll want to help us out with this?"

"If it concerns The Bogeyman, his realm, and The Third Heaven. I believe so."

Malach walked outside to the front. Carol watched him go as he closed the door. Outside, Malach stood still, his eyes closed. Though in his mind, he is contacting Darkous. Telling him of the recent news. From the sky comes down Darkous like a lightning bolt. His eyes intense. Malach opened his eyes and seen his Master before him.

"Master, You've come."

"I have. Let us enter inside and tell me more of this news you've spoken of."

Darkous and Malach enter the cabin and Carol sees Darkous for the first time. Frightened and excited at the same time, she stood up and faced him.

"Master, this woman is Carol Hunters. She's a supernatural reporter and has been aiding me on some information and I her."

"I recognize your features, Ms. Hunters." Darkous said.

"You do?"

"I know of you and how you wish to interview me."

"I... I didn't know."

"The interview can wait. I am here about what you said of The Bogeyman, his realm, and The Third Heaven. What of all this, Malach?"

"Carol knows of a secret society that calls themselves The Mythologists. They have in their possession a grimoire and are intending on using it to conjure Bogeyman and receive information as to enter his realm and The Third Heaven."

"This I will not allow." Darkous said. "Where is this group of theologians?"

"They're at the City Hall." Carol said. "They'll most likely be underneath the building for their meeting."

Darkous nodded.

"We will head there tonight. Confront these men and show them what true power is."

"Yes, Master."

Darkous walked out of the door and turned back to Malach and Carol.

"I will meet the two of you there."

"Yes, Master." Malach said. "We will be there."

Darkous flew up into the air and was gone.

The night fell upon the land and the moon glinted across the ground. Beneath the City Hall sat the Mythologists around a circular table and in the middle of the table laid the spell book. The lead Mythologist walked into the room and sat at the table.

"Gentlemen, we know why we're here this night and it is truly of great importance."

Outside of the City Hall walked Malach and Carol around the building toward the front doors. Malach had his sword prepared for battle as Carol noticed the door was being blocked by two men. She stopped Malach.

"What are you doing?"

"They granted me entrance into the meeting. Let me go in and when your Master arrives, you can enter then."

"I understand you. Be careful."

"I will."

Carol approached the two men. They stopped her from entering the doors.

"I was granted entrance to come to the meeting tonight."

"Let me check." The security guard said.

He contacted the Mythologists on the phone. He listened and put the phone away. He took several steps back and opened the door for Carol.

"You may enter."

"Thank you."

Carol entered City Hall and instantly could feel an energy going through the place. The energy was luring her downstairs to the meeting. She found the stairway and walked down to the floor. While walking down the stairs she could see the Mythologists at the circular table with the book in the middle. She walked toward the table and the Mythologists looked at her.

"Appears you've decided to come." The Mythologist said. "Wonderful."

"I couldn't miss something such as this."

"I can't agree with you more, ma'am."

She sat down at the table next to the Mythologist as he started to talk and go over the information that was given to them through the book.

"This book, lady and gentlemen, will grant us power beyond all belief of human reasoning. With this, we will possess true power."

Carol looked around for Malach, yet she didn't' see him. Outside, Malach killed the two security guards and entered City Hall. As he approached the stairwell, Darkous communicated with him through his mind.

"Wait." Darkous said. "Just wait."

"Yes, Master." Malach said. "I will wait on you."

The Mythologists opened the book and stopped on a page that referred to The Bogeyman. The Mythologist pointed at the spell and smiled to the others.

"This will give us power. I am thrilled for this."

He picked up the book and began to recite the spell. He spoke the spell in Latin. As he spoke, the lights began to flicker, he smiled.

"It is working!"

The lights flashed and the bulbs bursts above them. The Mythologists and Carol covered themselves from the falling glass. They looked around and could not see a thing. The room was in complete and thick darkness.

"What is going on in here?" The Mythologist said. "This isn't part of the ritual."

"No. It is not." said a voice within the darkness.

"Who is there?!" The Mythologist said. "Who is speaking to us all?!"

"You seem to be afraid."

"We fear what we do not understand because we know the power it possesses."

"Do you seek wisdom of the arts?"

"YES! WE SEEK WISDOM OF THE ARTS!." The Mythologists said altogether.

"Listen and listen good." said the voice.

"We are listening."

Within the thick darkness, they could feel an energy that was unknown to them, strange and uncomfortable, but their internal fear was becoming external.

"We're getting a little uneasy in this darkness."

"Do you fear it?"

"We do fear it. Because we do not fully understand its power."

"Why do you fear it?"

"We don't know who you are and why you've answered our request of appearance."

"The shadows are my domain. The darkness is where I dwell. Those who fear the darkness. Fear me."

The darkness faded away as the lights returned to its former state and atop the table in the middle of the Mythologists stood Darkous, staring at the lead Mythologist. Carol sat in awe of Darkous' feat as Malach entered the room with sword in hand. Darkous leaned in toward the lead Mythologist, seeing his fear.

"That is the wisdom you have received this night."

"Who the hell are you?!"

"I am Darkous, Keeper of the Cosmos and I am here to question you concerning your plots to conjure The Bogeyman, to enter the Dreamscape, and to make an attempt at entering The Third Heaven."

"Because we have to do so."

"Why would you even dare a feat that is impossible for humanity to partake?"

"Because humanity is lost to themselves. They have no guidance. No direction. They need it now or they will die amongst themselves in foolishness and ignorance."

Darkous stared at the lead Mythologist and kept his gaze toward him.

Searching the innermost parts of his heart and mind.

"You are not the true leader of this clan." Darkous said. "Where is your Master?"

"Our master?"

"You heard my words. Where is your Master?"

"Right there at the door."

Darkous turned and seen a man approaching them. Wearing a white cloak and his face hidden. He removed the hood and faced Darkous.

"Speak of your name, mortal."

"I am Dr. Geoff Hoff and this is my clan of Mythologists."

"Do you even understand what you are bargaining with, human. The feats that you have not even bared in your flesh?"

"That is why I sought out power and have discovered it."

"What do you mean?"

"I met a man, who possesses the powers of the dark arts. He aided me and gave me that spell book."

"Who is this man?"

"They call him Vernon Lance."

"Where is he?"

"He travels from church to church. Satanic churches and abandoned churches."

Darkous stepped down from the table and approached Hoff. He stood in front of him, towering over him in height. Hoff showed no fear in facing Darkous.

"What of this ritual to summon The Bogeyman, to enter the Dreamscape, and to break into The Third Heaven?"

"For you to know where The Bogeyman truly is located, you'll need to find a man they call the Spirit-Seeker. He will aid you in finding the answers you are seeking."

Darkous stared at Hoff and nodded before walking past him toward the door. Carol proceeds to follow him. Before exiting the room, Darkous turned back and looked at Hoff.

"Hoff. I give you this warning. If you ever make a breach into the cosmos, I will find you and show you what true power really is."

"I will look forward to it, Cosmos Keeper."

Darkous, Malach, and Carol left the room of the Mythologists, whom were frightened out of their seats. Hoff looked at them and shook his head.

"It seems there is more work to be done upon you gentlemen."

IV

DARKNESS SEEKS THE SPIRIT THAT SOUGHT IT

Leaving a small coffee shop is the Spirit-Seeker, Travis Vail. Returning to his base of operations, covered in books containing knowledge of the supernatural and mystic arts. Vail sat down at his desk and started reading through a grimoire, which contained information of conjuring deities from their dominions. The book was taken in an earlier event.

"I've never dealt with this before."

While he took sips of his coffee and read through the book, he hears a knocking at the door. Vail looked over toward the door and stood up from his desk. He walked to the door believing it to be someone who's stopped at the wrong location and is preparing himself mentally to tell them to go somewhere else.

"Who could this be?" Vail said. "I hope you've found the right place and not wasting time."

Vail opened the door and was immediately stunned. For Vail was staring into the eyes of Darkous himself. Darkous stood still and quiet. His eyes were locked on Vail's own.

"Travis Vail, I presume."

"Yes." Vail said. "You've come to the right place."

"Appears I have."

Vail let Darkous enter his place and closed the door afterwards. Vail returned to his desk while Darkous took a small look at the place. Seeing the relics that Vail has collected during his occult cases. From an ancient Indian burial relic to a photo with the name *Leta* attached to it.

"You have been out there much haven't you."

"I go where I'm needed."

"Very well, Mr. Vail." Darkous said turning toward Vail. "I need something of you at this appointed time."

"What do you need from me?" Vail said. "Cast out some demons, remove some spirits from a location? What will my assistance require?"

"I need you to help me find Vernon Lance."

Vail paused for a moment.

"Vernon Lance? As in the satanic priest Lance?"

"Yes."

"So, he's popped back up again."

"He has something that I require. It is of great importance to my mission and cause."

"Do tell me of your mission and cause, Mr.?"

"Darkous, Keeper of the Cosmos. But, you can call me Doctor Dark if you would prefer."

"Fair enough." Vail said. "I can tell from your aura that you're not human."

"I am not. I am an Astral entity."

"An Astral entity? So, you're basically from the outer realms."

"I am. Will you aid me in finding Vernon Lance?"

"I will. But, it might take a while to find him."

"We don't have a while to take, Mr. Vail." Darkous said. "We must confront him and take what he has in his possession."

"I can see you're in a rush to find him."

Vail grabbed his black coat and walked toward the front door. He looked at Darkous.

"I might know a few places to look."

They walked outside toward Vail's 1970 black Impala. Vail entered the car and he looked at Darkous, who was only standing there, staring at Vail and looking at his car.

"You're not going to get in the car?"

"No."

"Thought you need me to locate Lance."

"I do. Go to the place and I will meet you there."

"How will you do that exactly?"

"Because I can."

Darkous vanished into the air. Vail shook his head as he started the Impala.

"I guess this comes with the revelations."

Vail drove from his base down the streets. After a while, Vail stops by an old abandoned home. The home was once used by Lance and some of his satanic followers as a small base of operations to keep their rituals a secret from the outside world. Vail exited the car and walked toward the home. A small gust of wind blew across Vail. He nodded and turned around, seeing Darkous standing behind him.

"You found me." Vail said. "I am impressed."

"He's not here." Darkous said.

"How can you tell?"

"I searched the home while you parked your vehicle."

"That fast, you say?"

"Indeed. The energy within the home has eroded away."

Vail shook his head, walking back to his car. Darkous looked at him after glancing at the abandoned home.

"The next two locations you know of, what are they?"

"Well, one is an old storage facility and the other is an abandoned church."

Darkous nodded. "Let me do a search on the two and I will come back with the information needed in finding Vernon Lance."

"Sure thing." Vail said. "Search away."

Darkous flew up into the night sky, disappearing in the darkness above. Vail sat by his car, looking at his watch and counting the time.

"Thought he would be faster than that."

Darkous came down from the sky, landing in front of Vail. Vail chuckled a bit and started applauding Darkous' entrance.

"My, my." Vail said. "That was only a couple of seconds."

"Vernon Lance is located at the abandoned church. His aura surrounds the place. Let us stop him."

"Sure thing. I take it you will meet me there."

"I will." Darkous said before flying in the darkness again.

Vail entered the Impala and drove away. Making the rounds to reach the abandoned church, he finds himself being surrounded by individuals wearing black and scarlet robes with purple attachments standing outside in the street near the church.

"His lads are out here." Vail said. "Walking about in the damn street."

Vail honked his horn and the hooded figures turned toward him. He looked and noticed their eyes were glowing a bright red as they slowly made their way toward him. Vail prepared himself for the possible fight to come.

"First one to make a move gets sent to the Lake!"

As the hooded figures made their way toward Vail, a large gust of wind blows them across the street into a yard. Vail looked forward and could see Darkous standing in the street. The hoods stood up and surrounded Darkous in the street. Vail exited his car and reached into his pocket, pulling out his book of rituals.

"I can take these guys, Dark." Vail said.

"I know you can." Darkous said. "But, your energy is required in use against Lance. I will deal with these reprobates immediately."

"I would like to see this." Vail said. "Show them your power."

Darkous raised up both his arms toward the night sky as the moon shined above them. Thunder began to crack from the sky and lightning started to flash. From the sky came down a small tornado, blowing only through the street, picking up the hooded figures and tossing them around the yards. Clearing the street of the hoods, Darkous turned to Vail.

"May we finish what we've come to do."

"Sure. After you, Dark."

Darkous and Vail walked toward the church's front doors and Darkous blew them open with a gust of wind. Inside the abandoned church sat Vernon Lance and around him were four of his followers, dressed in black and scarlet. Lance looked at Vail and Darkous, smiling. His long wavy hair glowing with the moonlight, wearing his black clothing and black trench coat.

"How are you still around?" Vail wondered.

"Travis Vail makes his presence known to me once again." Lance said.

"I am deeply flattered."

"Don't take it as a friendly visit, Lance." Vail said. "We're here on some important causes."

"I can tell by the way your friend blew the doors open."

"Vernon Lance, give to me what you have taken from a realm you do not understand."

Lance laughed as he stood up from his seat and started walking toward Darkous and Vail. He pointed at Darkous, looking at his dark violet and black apparel.

"I recognize you from somewhere." Lance said. "Have we encountered one another before in time past?"

"This is our first meeting, Vernon Lance." Darkous said. "I can sense the aura of evil around you. You have consumed its power and believe you cannot be stopped."

"I can't be stopped, Dark One. No one can stop me with the power that I possess from the ha-Satan."

"You believe he cares for you, don't you?" Darkous said. "I will tell you, he cares for no one but himself and enjoys seeing others suffer to his own mischievous acts."

"How would you know what he thinks and does?"

"Because, unlike you, who speaks to a statue with a goat's head and a woman's body, I have spoken to the ha-Satan face to face. Angel to Astral. You have no idea as to what exists and transpires throughout the cosmos of this universe. Your little worship here and there will continue to go forward until you are stopped permanently."

"Is that why Vail has brought you here? To kill me?"

"No. I have come to take from you what doesn't belong to you."

"Which is what?" Lance said, pulling a small pouch from his coat pocket.

"What is that?" Vail said.

"Sand." Darkous said. "Dream sand. It belongs to The Sandman in order to enter the dreams of those who sleep."

"Sandman, you say. This is getting more and more open by the minute."

"This was given to me in a sale." Lance said. "I don't intend on

126

returning it to Sandman."

"You won't have to because I will."

Lance raised up his hand, shoving Vail against the wall. Darkous looked at the worshippers as they tried to attack him. One by one he grabbed them with a cloud of darkness and snapped their necks without the use of his hands. Lance noticed Darkous' power and giggled.

"When you said Astral, you were talking about yourself, huh?"

"I am." Darkous said. "What kind of spirit do you possess to wield such power?"

Lance showed a sinister grin.

"A greater kind."

Lance began reciting a spell, opening up a portal that released several demonic spirits to come out and they attacked Darkous. He fought back with the powers that he possesses while Vail got back to his feet. He glared at Lance.

"This is the kind of mess that you cause for the fun of it."

"I am a human with demonic intellect, Vail." Lance said. "Will you never understand that. I have true power in the palm of my hand. To do with as I please."

Vail looked around the church and noticed dozens of symbols that referred to portals across the world in different languages.

"You're using this place to conjure demons all across the world?"

"You're just now figuring that out. How slow has time made you, Spirit-Seeker."

Darkous defeated the demons and turned his attention toward Lance. He walked toward him. Lance tried to use his supernatural power against Darkous, but it has no effect on him.

"I know I can stop you, Dark One." Lance said. "I have the true power of darkness!"

"What do you know of darkness, mortal?" Darkous said. "You believe it to be of evil, yet, darkness was present before the light. I know all of this because I control the darkness and was commanded to keep it bound in its rightful place."

Darkous swooped over toward Lance and snatched away the pouch of sand from him. Lance looked and could see Darkous placing the pouch into his pocket.

"How dare you take something of such power away from one such as I." Lance said. "I possess demonic intellect! I am the kind of human that can change this world! A greater kind!"

"No." Darkous said. "You are not."

Darkous looked at Vail and nodded. "Send him to a prison somewhere. Do it quickly."

"I would love to." Vail said. "With great pleasure."

Vail opened up his book of rituals and turned the pages. While doing so, Lance began to recite a spell that started to suck the church up from the ground. A miniature earthquake was created as the wind started to blow like a hurricane and fires began to grow from the wooden floor.

"I got something for him." Vail said.

"Do it." Darkous said.

"Abba Pater, ex toto corde tuo et in virtute Spiritus Sancti , ut hoc mando tibi per gyrum dentium eius a daemonio in prisona ibi usque ad tempus statutum. Exite!"

Lance looked around and found himself being pulled into the ground by the spirits of Sheol. Lance screamed at Vail and Darkous with angry passion.

"This isn't the last of me, Vail! You hear me! I shall return!"

Lance was pulled and had vanished. The church and its location became silent as the wilderness. Vail looked around seeing no one inside but him and Darkous. He turned to Darkous and smiled.

"Looks like our work is done."

"It is." Darkous said. "I thank you for your support, Travis Vail."

"Anytime, Dark."

Darkous was preparing to leave, until Vail stopped him.

"I need to ask you of something."

"What do you want to ask?"

"All of this, Astrals, demons, gods, what more out there don't I know yet?"

"Travis Vail, I know you're new to all of this and I know the beginnings of your journey within the walls of paranormal investigation. It wasn't until you were visited by Kamagrauto that your whole world opened up. In time, you will see it was done for a much greater purpose. The team you've formed from the heavens. A purpose that will not only benefit those of the Spirit, but the future Kingdom to come as well."

"So, there's more of your kind out there? Astrals?"

"Yes."

"Any on the malevolent side of things?"

"There are. Some work for the forces of good. Others, the forces of evil. It's all for the balance of the universe."

They walked outside and Darkous looked up to the moon.

"I have to go, Travis Vail." Darkous said. "It was an honor to work alongside someone of your caliber."

"Whenever you require of my assistance, you know where to find me."

Darkous nodded as he disappeared. Vail returned to his Impala and drove away from the church that began to crumble apart.

Back in the Astral Dimension, Darkous looks at the pouch of sand. Analyzing it for the purpose of learning its power.

"With this, I shall find you, Bogeyman. I shall."

V

OUTER SLEEP

Searching for The Bogeyman's location, Darkous went through various attempts at finding him across the earth. He was nowhere to be found. Darkous later circled the earth's atmosphere to find him and he did not.

"He wouldn't take a break in the First Heaven. I know that to be true."

Darkous returned to his place in the Astral Dimension and studied the sand pouch. Beatrice appeared to him, seeing Darkous studying the pouch of sand.

"Is that dream sand?" Beatrice asked.

"It is." Darkous said. "It was earthbound."

"Last I knew, the Sandman wasn't walking about on the earth at this time."

"Because he's trapped inside the Dreamscape. The Bogeyman trapped him there to get out. This sand was in the possession of a Satan follower."

"Where's The ha-Satan now?"

"Going to and fro in the earth and walking upright in it as always."

"Can the sand give you a signal to finding Bogeyman?"

"No, it cannot. But, It can show me the entrance into the Dreamscape."

Darkous poured a tiny inch of the dream sand into the palm of his right hand and tossed it in the air above himself and Beatrice. The sand began to fall, but caught its own balance within the air. Flowing across the air by a cosmic current, the sand directed Darkous toward the entrance to the Dreamscape. Darkous looked and recognized the location the sand has chosen.

"The doorway is set within the Second Heaven."

"Are you sure about that?" Beatrice said. "I've never known there to be a door within the Second Heaven."

"I entered the doorway to Sheol through in the Second Heaven. Why not the doorway into the Dreamscape."

"Didn't seem to be a likely location is all I'm saying."

"I better be on my way to finding him. Contact me if something else comes up concerning the darkness and light issues."

Darkous left the Astral Dimension, traveling into the Second Heaven. Upon arriving in the Second Heaven, an archangel appears before him and stopped him in his tracks.

"Uriel." Darkous said. "What brings you to me?"

"Details concerning the matters of the darkness and the light."

"I was told about the issue by Michael. He gave me and advance notice."

"True. Though, you have been so concerned with the matters of The Bogeyman and he had diverted you from the real cause of concern."

"You mean to tell me that The Bogeyman is nothing more than a diversion set upon me? By who?"

"Who do you think, Darkous."

Darkous nodded.

"Should I let The Bogeyman be and Heaven will take care of him?"

"No. You have already made this your mission currently. After you have dealt with Bogeyman, you will receive a call and you will answer the call."

"Who will contact me afterwards?"

"You will know his voice."

Uriel disappeared before Darkous' eyes. He looked around for him and couldn't find Uriel. He set his attention toward the Dreamscape entrance and took some more of the dream sand and scattered it through the vacuum of outer space. The sand took some rounds and revealed the doorway to Darkous.

"There it is." Darkous said.

The doorway to the Dreamscape opened and Darkous could see the brightening colors pouring out as if it was a place of peace. Darkous made his way toward the door and could feel and aura surrounding him.

He entered the doorway and stepped on the grounds of the Dreamscape. Standing in front of him was The Bogeyman. Holding a set of blades ranging from a sword to a scythe. His eyes held a sense of torment within them as his stare could send a human into utter shock.

"You decided to appear to me without making a move?" Darkous said.

"You're in my realm now." The Bogeyman said. "Are you afraid of me, Shrouded One?"

"No. The thing is, after we have our battle, you will fear me."

"We will see about that."

VI

IN THE DREAM, WE SEE OUR CALLING

Darkous and Bogeyman engage in a battle of the powers of the realms. Darkous using various attacks against Bogeyman, whom used his sword and scythe to slash away at the darkness that Darkous would conjure up against him. Bogeyman laughed at Darkous.

"Your power isn't as strong within this realm. You're in my domain now!"

"You underestimate the power of an Astral entity." Darkous said. "We have more than what was given to us."

Darkous waved his hand to his side. Bogeyman was confused at the matter. Back on earth, Malach looked around his cabin and could feel and energy calling to him. He grabbed his sword and stepped outside and looked up, suddenly he disappeared from his home and appeared standing next to Darkous in the Dreamscape. Malach looked at Darkous, who turned to him and nodded.

"I need a little bit of your assistance on this one, Malach."

"Whatever you say, Master." Malach said. "So, this is The Bogeyman?"

"It is. In the flesh."

"Rather in the dream." Bogeyman said. "This will be fun for me, but tormenting for the two of you."

Darkous and Malach attacked Bogeyman at once. Ranging from side attacks to attacks from behind and front. Darkous fired a sphere of dark matter toward Bogeyman, knocking him back into the Dreamscape gates.

"What kind of place is this?" Malach said.

"They call it the Dreamscape." Darkous said. "This is Bogeyman's domain and the Sandman's."

"The Sandman is here?"

"I believe him to be. We'll have to release him from his prison."

The Bogeyman began conjuring illusions of himself and demons of the dreams to attack Darkous and Malach. Both using their abilities against the illusions to find Bogeyman within them. Darkous blew the illusions away with a gust of wind from his hands and grabbed Bogeyman by the head, slamming him into the ground of the Dreamscape, creating a sound resembled to a bell being rung.

Malach ,take this!" Darkous said giving Malach the pouch of sand.

"What am I supposed to do with this?"

"Use it to find the Sandman. He will help us trap Bogeyman back into his prison."

Malach looked around at the tall buildings within the Dreamscape and could see a castle ahead.

"Toss the sand into the air, Malach!" Darkous said. "The sand will lead you directly to the Sandman!"

"Yes, Master." Malach said throwing the sand into the air above the battle.

The sand rotated in the air, circling itself twice before moving across the sky, heading toward the castle. Malach ran after the sand, following its trail. Darkous and Bogeyman continued their battle with Darkous taking Bogeyman's sword and snapping it within his hands.

"Face me with your hands, dream demon."

Malach arrived at the castle, which the sand made a turn toward its lower doors connected to an underground area. Malach followed as the sand slid through the crack of the door. Malach used his sword to open the door. He continued to follow the sand until it stopped at a dark cell. Malach looked inside and seen a man sitting on the floor.

"Seems my sand has returned to me." The man said inside the cell.

"Are you the Sandman?" Malach said.

"I am. Thank you for bringing it to me."

"Me and my Master need your help right now."

"I am aware of the current circumstance. Lead the way, young one."

The cell doors busted open as the Sandman walked through. Malach stood quietly and stared at the Sandman.

"Lead, young one."

Malach led the Sandman to the outside where they could see Darkous and Bogeyman continuing their battle. Malach held his sword tightly, preparing to run into the battle, but Sandman placed his hand across Malach's chest.

"I need to assist my Master." Malach said.

"Do not run into the battle." Sandman said. "Let us deal with The Bogeyman."

Darkous slammed Bogeyman, but was kicked in the chest. He looked across the open area, seeing Sandman walking towards him and Bogeyman. Darkous released a wind of darkness, slamming Bogeyman back onto the ground.

"Keeper of the Cosmos." Sandman said. "I will finish this battle."

"By all means."

Darkous moved out of the way as the Sandman approached Bogeyman. Bogeyman, who stood up from the ground faced Sandman in the eyes. He released a small gesture of laughter.

"They set you free?!"

"They did and not I will place you in your eternal chamber."

Sandman tossed his sand toward Boegeyman, entering his eyes as he fell to the ground. The ground beneath his feet opened up, revealing a horde of shadow men as they grabbed Bogeyman by his limbs and dragged him into the ground. Bogeyman yelled for repentance.

"You will not be given repentance this day, dream demon." Darkous said. "Now, go into your prison in peace."

The ground closed itself with Bogeyman inside. The area was calm, Sandman turned toward Darkous and Malach.

"I thank you once more for releasing me from my prison."

"It was our duty to restore the balance of the Dreamscape." Darkous said.

As the Sandman spoke to them, Darkous glared up into the air. He could hear a voice calling to him. A voice only few can hear. Darkous listened and he recognized the voice he could hear. Malach looked at him and could feel there was a communication taking place.

"Master, what is it?" Malach said.

"I am needed." Darkous said. "My Master demands my presence."

Darkous returned Malach back onto earth at his home. Meanwhile, Darkous made his way toward the voice that called to him. The voice came from the Third Heaven.

DARKOUS OF THE ASTRALS SHALL RETURN.

NEXT BOOK IN

THE DARK TITAN UNIVERSE SAGA....

A BOOK RETURNING TO THE
RESISTANCE AND THE PROTECTORS
AS IT BEGINS A NEW TRILOGY!

ABOUT THE AUTHOR

Ty'Ron W. C. Robinson II is the author of several works of fiction. Including the *Dark Titan Universe Saga* series (*Dark Titan Knights, The Resistance Protocol, Tales of the Scattered, Tales of the Numinous, Day of Octagon, Crossbreed, Heaven's Called*), *The Haunted City Saga* series, the *Symbolum Venatores* series, and the *Frightened!* series.

Also of other books (*Lost in Shadows, The Book of The Elect, etc.*) and One-Shot short stories.

More information pertaining to the author and stories can be found at darktitanentertainment.com.

Twitter: @TyRonRobinsonII
Instagram: @tyronrobinsonii

Twitter: @DarkTitan_
Instagram: @darktitanentertainment
Facebook: @DarkTitanEnt

CPSIA information can be obtained
at www.ICGtesting.com
Printed in the USA
LVHW090319021120
670424LV00036B/694/J